Don't miss the other books in
the Book Scavenger series:

A *New York Times* Bestseller

An Indie Next List Pick

A Junior Library Guild Selection

An NCTE Notable Children's Book
in the Language Arts

A Bank Street College Best Book of the Year

A Scripps National Spelling Bee
Great Words, Great Works List Selection

A PW Best Book for Summer

An Amazon Best Book of the Year

A Triple Crown Award Winner

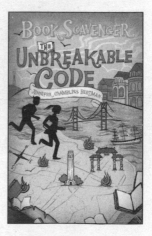

A *New York Times* Bestseller

A Junior Library Guild Selection

"Brisk, bookish good fun for puzzle and
code lovers." —*Kirkus Reviews*

"A successful sequel . . . Readers who
loved the first volume will find this
follow-up even more satisfying."
—*School Library Journal*

THE ALCATRAZ ESCAPE

Jennifer Chambliss Bertman

WITH ILLUSTRATIONS BY Sarah Watts

SQUARE FISH

Christy Ottaviano Books

HENRY HOLT AND COMPANY • NEW YORK

SQUARE
FISH

An imprint of Macmillan Publishing Group, LLC
175 Fifth Avenue, New York, NY 10010
mackids.com

Our books may be purchased in bulk for promotional, educational, or
business use. Please contact your local bookseller or the Macmillan Corporate
and Premium Sales Department at (800) 221-7945 ext. 5442 or by email at
MacmillanSpecialMarkets@macmillan.com.

Library of Congress Control Number: 2017957741
ISBN 978-1-250-30870-2 (paperback)   ISBN 978-1-62779-964-5 (ebook)

Originally published in the United States by Christy Ottaviano Books/
Henry Holt and Company
First Square Fish edition, 2019
Book designed by April Ward
Square Fish logo designed by Filomena Tuosto

1 3 5 7 9 10 8 6 4 2

AR: 5.8 / LEXILE: 860L

To Cade and Kayla Chambliss

THE ALCATRAZ ESCAPE

CHAPTER 1

IF ONE OF Errol Roy's fans had passed him on the street, they wouldn't have known who he was. With the wispy white hair that covered most of his head and nearly reached his shoulders, and his long cottony beard tinged with yellow, he was more likely to be mistaken for Santa Claus than for himself. Nobody knew what Errol Roy looked like, but his books were recognized around the world.

On this day in mid-March, the author stood at the bay window of his San Francisco apartment.

"It's been a long road, Dash," Errol said aloud to his cat, who was stretched across the windowsill. Dash swatted his tail in response.

Errol was thinking about his personal favorite of his own books. He doubted any of his readers could correctly guess which it was out of the twenty-some mysteries he'd written. It was arguably the most obscure: *A Body in the Alley*. A horrible title. Maybe that was why it hadn't sold well.

In *A Body in the Alley*, Mickey Jones is a crook who continuously finds himself in the wrong place at the wrong time but finally pulls off the bank heist of his dreams. At the book's close, he sails into the sunset while the detective on his trail watches him get away. The book ends with this line:

The boat disappeared over the horizon, rings spreading behind like a peacock fanning its tail.

Errol Roy had written millions of sentences in his lifetime, but that was one he had never forgotten. It wasn't so much the writing he was fond of, but the image it painted and the feeling of freedom it gave him. It was an ending Errol had always wanted to try, but it turned out critics and readers didn't like it when their detective hero lost.

Dash sat up and stretched out a paw to tap his owner, as though encouraging Errol to look up. The view below was of a hillside gouged from its quarry days, now covered in vines and shrubs. The scene straight ahead could be a San Francisco postcard.

On a crisp, clear day you could see all the way from the Golden Gate Bridge to the tiny stump of Gull Island, which had been on the news because two kids and their teacher had found buried treasure there. And if the bay was a stage, then front and center was Alcatraz.

Errol Roy rested his eyes on the famous former

prison, which had had a reputation for being inescapable. Now Alcatraz was a popular tourist destination, attracting travelers from around the world, and soon it would be the setting of the latest cockamamie game creation by Garrison Griswold, the city's beloved book publisher and game enthusiast.

Errol sighed.

Last fall, his most recent mystery had been published to great fanfare, not that he had participated in any of it. He never did. That decision had started out as a spontaneous choice made decades ago, which grew into his reputation. His "branding," as the publishing industry termed it today. The most popular mysteries in America, written by a man who was himself a mystery. Once, he had stood in line at the grocery store behind a woman who had piled produce, a plastic tray of muffins, and his latest paperback onto the conveyor belt. She and the cashier had had a lively discussion about his books, never realizing the author stood right beside them.

Errol had planned for his most recent book to be the final of his career, but when Garrison Griswold announced this new game, he knew it was time to tell the last story he had in him. There would be considerable risk, but it rankled him to leave loose ends dangling.

He was a novelist, after all.

"It's time, Dash," he said, and turned from the view.

The cat meowed, as though hoping his owner meant it was time for dinner, and dropped to the floor with a gentle thud. When the man crossed the room to his computer desk instead of the kitchen, Dash meowed again. His tail quirked into a question mark.

Errol lowered himself into his chair and opened his laptop. He bent over his keyboard and began to type.

CHAPTER 2

EMILY CRANE and her best friend, James, ran along a dirt alley closed in by a graffiti-covered fence on one side and a vine-covered fence on the other. The path cut horizontally across a hill. Emily couldn't see the two- and three-story buildings above and below them, but she knew they were there.

"They're going to catch up to us," James panted.

Emily looked back. The path behind them was empty, all the way to the arched trellis they'd entered under. Their feet pounded past weeds that grew to their ears. An enormous shrub spilled over the top of a fence like it was trying to jump into the alley and make a break for it. The path curved, and there was the exit back onto a street in Emily and James's San Francisco neighborhood.

"We're almost there—we can make it!" Emily shouted, but a hooded figure jumped in front of the exit and blocked their way. Emily hadn't anticipated that they'd be stopped from the front. She and James stumbled a bit, trying to change course and run back the way they'd come. Before they could fully turn around, there was a soft pop, and purple powder splattered across their shirts.

"Found you!" their friend Maddie crowed, her sweatshirt hood falling back off her head. She was nearly a head taller than both of them, so when she triumphantly held up the plastic bottle of colored cornstarch and squeezed, more violet dust rained down over Emily and James.

"You're out," Maddie said.

"Aw, man!" James stomped a foot in mock disgust. The purple-dusted black cowlick atop his head, which James affectionately called Steve, bobbed indignantly. "You could have let the birthday boy win, you know."

Maddie rolled her eyes. "Right. Like I'm going to do that."

James aimed his squeeze bottle at Maddie, and a puff of green powder blasted toward her. She jumped aside so only her shoulder got hit. Laughing, she said, "Too late! Purple team still won!"

Footsteps came up behind them, and Emily turned to see their other friends, Devin, Kevin, Nisha, and Vivian, coming down the path. Devin had been on their team, but he and his twin brother had blasted each other with powder within minutes of the game starting, leaving only Emily and James to fend for Team Green.

"I told you I could beat them to the end of the path, Vivian," Maddie called over.

Vivian frowned—she was more comfortable doing the correcting than being corrected—but she nodded and said, "Good job." Vivian looked even more crisp and polished than usual, being the only one of the group without green or purple splattered across her face and clothes.

"Do we win anything?" Nisha asked, removing her glasses. She attempted to clean them with her shirt, but only succeeded in smearing green dust across the lens.

"Here." James plucked Nisha's glasses from her hands. "The back of my shirt is clean." He tugged a corner of fabric forward and rubbed furiously, then handed them back. "Your team wins my undying admiration— even you, Maddie."

Maddie and James had a competitive history that dated back to their elementary school days, long before Emily had known either of them. Recently the rivalry had taken on a friendly tone. Which still felt totally weird, if you asked Emily.

"You can keep the T-shirts, too," James added.

Nisha lifted her shirt like an old-timey lady curtseying in a petticoat. She was the smallest in their group, and her shirt hung to her knees. "My mom's always telling me to wear more dresses."

Maddie peeled off her shirt from over her sweatshirt. "The winners also get first choice for pizza," she declared.

James shrugged. "Sure. Speaking of, let's eat!"

He led the group back the way he and Emily had come. The alley connected to a very narrow, vertical public garden that was broken into tiers, with stairs zigzagging the slope. The group climbed the stairs, weaving around rosebushes and daylilies until they reached the halfway point, where James's mom sat on one of two benches that faced the San Francisco Bay.

His mom held two pizza boxes in one hand and slid her sunglasses onto her head with the other. "Wow . . . ," she said, taking in their green- and purple-stained faces, arms, legs, and clothes. "Your parents are going to kill me."

"It washes out, Mom. I told you," James said.

His hand darted forward and his mom yelped, trying to dodge, but James was too fast and wiped a purple streak on her cheek.

She laughed. "You're lucky it's your birthday," she said.

Maddie's team chose their slices; then the others took their turn. After distributing napkins and drinks, James's mom balanced the empty boxes on one hand and hiked the stairs that continued up the hill. She called back, "Parent pickup in forty-five minutes!"

Emily sat on a bench with James and Nisha; Maddie and Vivian sat on the other bench that was on the tier below them. The twins stretched out on the five stairs in between.

Everyone ate quietly until Maddie asked, "Is

everyone trying out?" She straddled the bench so she could face Vivian and the rest of the group sitting up the hill behind the two girls.

They all knew she was talking about Unlock the Rock, Mr. Griswold's upcoming game. From where they sat eating their lunch, they could see Alcatraz down below on the water, framed in the corridor between buildings on either side.

Vivian folded her napkin and pressed it to her lips. "My parents won't let me miss my flute lesson, plus it's a school night."

"Failed the entry puzzle," Devin announced. "Big time."

"You sound proud," Maddie said.

"It was a pretty spectacular failing."

His brother nodded in agreement. "If they gave grades for failing, he would have gotten an A-plus."

Maddie rolled her eyes and turned to Emily and James. "You two are probably automatically entered, being on Mr. Griswold's teen advisory board and everything," she said.

"Do you know what he's planning?" Nisha asked.

"We don't know anything." Emily spoke up while James finished chewing. "At least no more than what he told all of us when we were painting Hollister's bookstore: It will be like an escape room set on Alcatraz."

"And we aren't automatically entered," James added. "We told Mr. Griswold we wanted to play the game, and he said we'd be treated like every other book scavenger. I solved my entry puzzle and got a ticket yesterday." Each Book Scavenger user was assigned a unique entry puzzle, so no two people had the same one.

"Have you done yours yet?" James asked Emily.

She shook her head and took a bite of pizza, unable to look James in the eye. The truth was she had attempted her puzzle, but she'd gotten the wrong answer. She had two more tries left, but she didn't want to admit to her friends that she was struggling.

James squinted at her, and Steve tilted skeptically on top of his head. "I thought you would have been one of the first entered."

Emily held a crumpled paper towel to her mouth as she swallowed her bite, trying to buy herself some time. "I keep meaning to do it and then something comes up. Like last weekend I was going to, but then my parents wanted to take that hike in the Presidio, and I was too tired when we got home."

That was all true—going on the hike and being tired—and James nodded like he understood, but he still had that pinched, pensive look on his face that made her wonder if he could tell she wasn't being completely honest.

"You'd better get on it, because the game's Wednesday. There are only a few days left," James said.

"You can always hunt for a golden ticket if you can't solve your puzzle," Maddie added.

A week ago Mr. Griswold had posted a video to the Book Scavenger site in which he'd announced that in a nod to his nickname, "the Willy Wonka of book publishing," he was offering fifty golden tickets for hopeful attendees who hadn't been able to solve the entry puzzles. The tickets could be found inside fifty copies of the book *Infinite City: A San Francisco Atlas*, which were hidden through Book Scavenger across the Bay Area. The day Mr. Griswold announced their existence, seven golden tickets were found, and more had been claimed every day since.

Nisha and Vivian laughed good-naturedly at the idea of Emily needing to use a golden ticket to gain her

GRISWOLD'S GOLDEN TICKET
You're Invited
to Unlock the Rock

entry, but Emily wasn't sure if Maddie had been joking. Was she trying to get under her skin, as usual, or could she tell Emily was stumped by a puzzle?

"Is that what you're doing, Maddie?" James retorted. "Using a golden ticket?"

"I already solved my puzzle," Maddie said. "It was super easy." She said these last words like she was throwing them at Devin, trying to rub in the fact that she had passed and he'd failed. He shrugged in response, unfazed, but Emily slumped even more, feeling miserable to be struggling with something Maddie had found easy. That it was something Emily had a reputation for doing well made it sting even worse.

"I'm not sure I'll try out," Nisha said. "I've heard Alcatraz is haunted."

"Oh, it is," Maddie agreed. "I took the tour with my mom and her boyfriend a couple of years ago. It's super creepy. When it was a prison, the worst criminals were sent there. Murderers and psychopaths—"

"They weren't *all* murderers and psychopaths," James interjected. "I've taken the tour, too, and I remember our guide said some convicts were sent there not because their crimes were so awful, but because they were disruptive prisoners or had a habit of trying to escape."

Considering the island ahead of them, Emily could see how it had gotten the reputation for being inescapable. It was small but formidable. The perimeter of the island looked steep and rocky, so even if you were able to get out of the massive cell house that crowned the top, it would surely be daunting or perhaps impossible to get down to the water. And if you managed that, well, then you were in the middle of a cold bay known for strong currents that could pull you out to the Pacific Ocean, not to mention the occasional shark.

"Maybe the prisoners weren't *all* violent and dangerous," Maddie said. "But some were, and people *did* die on Alcatraz."

"Stop trying to scare Nisha," Vivian scolded. "There are tons of creepy stories about Alcatraz, but that doesn't mean it's haunted."

"That's not very reassuring," Nisha said.

Emily nudged her knee against Nisha's. "This is Mr. Griswold we're talking about. With him in charge, any ghosts on Alcatraz will end up falling into line like the ones at Hogwarts."

"Emily's right," Vivian said. "You should go if you can, Nisha. I wish I could. It's guaranteed to be fun—not scary. And besides, you'll all be together, right?"

"Right," everyone said in unison, except for Devin, who happily sang out, "Wrong!" and Emily, who shoved her last bite of pizza in her mouth.

CHAPTER 3

A BOLDFACED *READY?* taunted Emily from her laptop screen. Ever since the conversation about Unlock the Rock at James's birthday party earlier that day, she'd been feeling the nagging pressure to solve her entry puzzle, if only she could figure out how. Her index finger hovered over the Enter key, but she couldn't summon the nerve to actually press down and select "yes" to reveal her puzzle once again and start the timer.

This was ridiculous. Emily pushed her laptop onto her bed and stood up. She paced her room, glancing every so often at her computer screen. It was a *puzzle.* She'd solved a billion Book Scavenger puzzles and had never freaked out about them before, but her confidence had been rattled. She'd been so certain she had the right answer the first time she attempted to solve this puzzle, and now the pressure of knowing she only had two chances left—and imagining the embarrassment if she had to admit she couldn't do it—was getting to her. Emily spun on her heel and stalked down the hallway to the kitchen. She needed brain food.

Her brother, Matthew, was looking at his reflection in the microwave, messing with his off-kilter Mohawk, which had been newly dyed.

"Green again?" Emily reached over his shoulder and plucked a banana from the fruit bowl that sat on top of the microwave. It was covered in brown spots but she peeled it anyway, flicking the mushy top into the trash.

"Saint Patrick's Day," Matthew said by way of explanation.

"You look like you have grass sprouting across your head," Emily said.

Her snark didn't faze Matthew. He turned side to side to see his hair from all angles. "Then it's symbolic for spring, too. Maybe I'll add some daisies."

Emily couldn't tell if he was serious. Probably not, but she snapped, "So you can win a Most Ridiculous Hair contest?"

She regretted her words immediately. One of the things she admired about her brother was how he didn't seem to care what anyone thought.

"Sorry," she said. "I'm just stuck on a problem I can't solve."

"Homework?" Matthew asked.

Emily shook her head. "It's . . ." She'd been reluctant to admit to her friends that she was having trouble, but this was Matthew. There was less to lose confiding in her brother, and he wasn't into Book Scavenger anymore, so he wouldn't think less of her for not being able to solve a puzzle. And even if he did, she was used to him teasing her. "It's the puzzle for Unlock the Rock."

"Seriously? It's that hard?"

Emily was touched that Matthew would assume the puzzle must be hard rather than she wasn't smart.

"Want me to take a look?" Matthew asked.

Emily rolled her eyes. "Very funny."

Her brother might have liked doing puzzles for fun, but he wasn't competitive about them like Emily. She doubted he'd take it as seriously as she would. Besides, if she couldn't solve this puzzle on her own, then she didn't deserve to go to Unlock the Rock.

She was halfway back to her room when Matthew called out, "You know I was serious, right? About helping?"

"I only have two more chances to solve it. I can't blow it by goofing around."

She looked back, surprised to see a hurt expression on Matthew's face, though it was quickly replaced by his normal, easygoing smile. He shrugged. "Suit yourself. There's more than one puzzle person in this family, you know."

Ignoring him, Emily slipped back into her room. She woke up her laptop but couldn't bring herself to try again just yet. Instead she went to the forums to see what people were saying about the game.

Skimming the new messages posted in the "Unlock

the Rock" thread, her eyes landed on a username she recognized: Bookacuda.

"*He's* coming?" Emily muttered to herself. Bookacuda was the youngest Sherlock-level player in the United States. Also the most arrogant and obnoxious. He didn't live in San Francisco—he didn't even live in California, if she remembered correctly. He was an eighth grader who lived in . . .

Nebraska? Emily squinted at her screen to make sure she was reading Bookacuda's profile right. He was going to travel all the way from Nebraska for the game? It wasn't unheard of for people to do that for one of Mr. Griswold's games, of course, but since this game was the lead-up to the grand reopening of Hollister's store, it seemed like more of a local thing.

Emily scrolled through the various messages in the forum about Unlock the Rock. When she got to a post from a Nancy Drew–level player—the second lowest level—exclaiming *The entry puzzle was so much FUN!!!!!!* Emily slapped her comforter. "That's it!"

She opened the Unlock the Rock entry page and clicked "yes" before she could overthink it any more.

A ten-minute timer started the countdown. She saw the same puzzle as before. Emily knew there were other people who probably copied theirs down or took a picture in order to work on it outside the time limit, but Emily wasn't that kind of player. If the challenge was to solve a puzzle within a given amount of time, that was

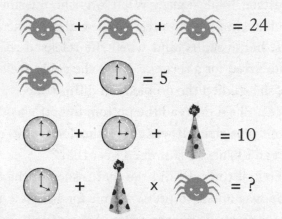

$$\text{🕷} + \text{🕷} + \text{🕷} = 24$$

$$\text{🕷} - \text{🕰} = 5$$

$$\text{🕰} + \text{🕰} + \text{🎉} = 10$$

$$\text{🕰} + \text{🎉} \times \text{🕷} = ?$$

what she was going to do. It felt like cheating to do it any other way.

When she'd first attempted to solve this the other day, Emily had gotten the answer 15. The puzzle had seemed so easy, but when she'd submitted her solution, the computer had spit out the message: *I'm sorry, that's incorrect. You have two chances remaining.*

Reviewing the puzzle again with fresh eyes, Emily *still* couldn't believe fifteen wasn't the right answer. She walked through her logic.

"Three spiders equals twenty-four," she muttered to herself. "Which means a spider stands for the number eight. If eight minus a clock is five, then the clock is equal to three. Three plus three plus a hat equals ten . . . so the hat must be four. Which means three plus four plus eight equals . . ." Emily scribbled the math in her notebook.

"Fifteen." She sighed. What was she missing? This seemed so simple. She pressed the palms of her hands against her eyeballs, and when she released them, her vision blurred for a second. When she could see straight again, she studied the problem, and this time—

"Ha!" She'd misread the bottom line. It wasn't three plus four plus eight. It was three plus four *times* eight.

"I can't believe I skimmed over that."

The first time she did the math, she got the answer 56. She was about to press submit for her new answer when she remembered the order of operations. You were supposed to do multiplication before addition.

"*Multiply*," she scolded herself. She redid the math:

$$3 + 4 \times 8 = ?$$
$$4 \times 8 = 32$$
$$3 + 32 = 35$$

"Thirty-five! Thirty-five, thirty-five, thirty-five," Emily started chanting to herself in a made-up tune. She double-checked her work, but she knew it was right this time. She couldn't believe she'd missed that multiplication symbol. That was what happened when you were overconfident and rushed through a problem.

Emily typed 35 into the answer space and pressed "Enter." The computer replied:

I'm sorry, that's incorrect.
You have one chance remaining.

CHAPTER 4

THE ELEVATOR in Errol Roy's apartment building was old and narrow and dark. The door was an elaborate iron gate, like something you'd see in front of a haunted mansion, and it made him feel trapped in a cage. For years he'd taken the stairs instead, but that was harder at his age. Today he carried a large sack piled high with cans of cat food and towed a rolling cart holding multiple containers of kitty litter, so he rode up the elevator with his eyes closed and pictured a beach he used to visit in Brazil.

When he arrived at his floor, he slid the metal grate open, which made a terrible racket echoing down the hall. Hoisting the paper sack up an inch, he dragged his squeaking roller cart to his apartment two doors down.

Errol fumbled to get his keys out of his pocket. The door across from his opened, but he acted like he hadn't heard a thing.

"Oh, hello, Ernie!" His neighbor Valerie called to him like he was across a gigantic room instead of only a couple of feet away. Long ago, before he'd moved to this apartment building, he'd blurted out the name "Ernie" in a moment of panic when he'd been worried someone might connect his name with his books. From then on he'd stuck with "Ernie" for any in-person encounters, to help keep his privacy.

"Stocking up on kitty supplies?" Valerie asked.

He didn't have to face her to know his neighbor had stepped from her apartment and was craning her neck to see in his bag. Valerie seemed to feel a kinship with Errol/Ernie because they were the oldest people in their building. At least he assumed they were—he didn't make it a point to seek out his neighbors.

Errol unlocked his front door instead of greeting Valerie, hoping to signal that he wasn't interested in a chat.

"Did you hear they'll be repainting our hallway next week?" she asked.

He reluctantly turned. As much as he wanted to disappear, it felt too rude even for him to enter his apartment without so much as acknowledging her question. Today Valerie wore a green sweat suit. She rotated among the colors of the rainbow. Not that Errol was one to comment on clothing. He always wore what he considered his writer uniform: loose pants cinched by a belt under his rotund belly and one of five San Francisco sweatshirts he'd picked up at the souvenir shops that populated Fisherman's Wharf.

"I hope the fumes aren't too bad," Valerie said. "I asked the super if they'd be using low-VOC paint, because you know I get those headaches. . . ." She prattled on while Errol stared at a scuff mark shaped like Oklahoma on the beige walls. He hadn't known their building would be painted, but now that he studied the walls, it seemed long overdue.

". . . and so if you need any broccoli, I have plenty extra."

Errol darted a look to Valerie's wide, encouraging smile. He wasn't sure when or where the one-sided conversation had jumped tracks to vegetables.

"I'm fine, thank you." Errol turned back to his door, restraining himself from shoving it open and hurrying inside.

Valerie meant well. He thought she worried about him because he didn't have family and spent most of his time by himself. And Errol supposed he should be glad for that—to have somebody check in on him every now and then. But what he really appreciated was that Valerie, for the most part, understood he liked to be left alone.

"All right, dear. Let me know if you change your mind." Valerie called him dear even though he was likely older than her. It was actually one of her quirks he was fond of.

He opened his door and wheeled the litter in ahead of him.

"Did you get another cat?" Valerie asked. "That's quite a lot you have there."

"No, I'm . . ." Errol studied the litter, not yet wanting to tell her he was planning a trip. Orchestrating something in real life was more complicated than he'd expected. He was used to controlling fictional characters and outcomes.

"Must have been on sale," Valerie said, finishing his sentence for him.

Errol nodded and smiled absently in her general direction, then stepped into his apartment.

CHAPTER 5

BY SUNDAY MORNING, Emily was beginning to panic. She needed to earn her way into Unlock the Rock before Wednesday, which left her with three days and only one last chance to solve that stupid puzzle. What if she couldn't figure it out? What would she do then?

She hated to admit it, but she needed to find a golden ticket. At least to hang on to for backup—to make sure she'd be participating in Unlock the Rock one way or the other. If she solved the entry puzzle, then she could give the golden ticket to Devin and act like that was why she'd found it in the first place.

Win-win.

But when Emily clicked on the golden-ticket map, she discovered there were only nine left, and several were not in the city. The two closest were hidden at the Grace Cathedral and in the Mission. The clue for the book hidden in the Mission looked like the easier of the two to solve, and she'd had enough of challenging puzzles, thank you very much, so she went with that.

ONYZLFGERRGIVPGBEVBA

Hint: A = N = A

Using the hint, Emily started by plugging an *A* where she saw an *N*, and *N* where she saw an *A*.

OAYZLFGERRGIVPGBEVBN

The change wasn't drastic, but she realized that swapping the same letters for each other was probably significant. It made her wonder if this substitution cipher could be like one she'd seen before, where you folded the alphabet in half to create your key:

A	B	C	D	E	F	G	H	I	J	K	L	m
N	O	P	Q	R	S	T	U	V	W	X	Y	Z

Emily plugged in the letters to decode the following message:

Balmy Street Victorion

It worked! Emily did an online search for "Balmy Street" and, sure enough, one existed in San Francisco. A Victorian was an old-fashioned building style, so a house on Balmy Street must be where she had to go to find the golden ticket.

Now all she had to do was convince her family of the urgency of the situation.

Emily ran into the family room and announced, "We need to go to the Mission!"

Matthew was bent over a folding table, carefully maneuvering LEGO characters into a beach scene he'd set up on the makeshift white background that he used to film his stop-motion videos. Mr. Crane was stretched out on the couch under the bay window and flipped a page in the book he was reading. Mrs. Crane studied photos she was editing on the computer.

Emily cleared her throat. "I said: We need to go to the Mission!"

"We'll go one day soon," her dad replied.

"I mean now. Can we go now? There's a book I need to find before someone else does," she pleaded.

"You're still declaring books on Book Scavenger?" Matthew asked. He lowered the swing-arm lamp to focus the light more closely on his miniature movie set. "I thought you already advanced to Dupin level."

For a while Emily had been obsessed with trying to advance from Miss Marple level to Auguste Dupin level, and the speediest way to do that was to declare books on the website before you downloaded a clue. Declaring a book made it worth double the points, but the downside was that declared books were flagged on the website so everyone knew they were now worth more to whoever found them first. Matthew was right—she'd already advanced to Dupin, and it would take a long time and a lot of found books before she moved to the level above that.

"This isn't a declared book. It's for something else," she said. "The book is near someplace called Balmy Street and—"

"Balmy Street?" Their mom looked up.

"Yeah," Emily said hesitatingly, not sure if the fact that her mom recognized it was a good thing or a bad thing.

"That's been on our list for ages, David." Emily's parents maintained a blog and were writing a book about their goal of living once in each of the fifty states.

"It is?" Emily asked. "Why?"

"Street art," her dad replied. "It's an alley lined with murals by a variety of artists. The Mission is known for having a lot of murals, but Balmy Street is one of the most famous spots."

Matthew nodded. "Sweet."

Mrs. Crane stretched her neck side to side and pushed back from the computer. "I've been sitting way too long. I can take a break." She tugged her camera bag free from under the computer table, double-checking that the equipment she wanted was inside.

"I'm going, too," Matthew announced.

"I'll check the bus schedule!" Emily ran back to her room and laptop, relieved that her family was on board. She tried to ignore the chip of guilt she felt about avoiding the entry puzzle and doing this instead.

She wasn't giving up. Finding a golden ticket was simply good strategy.

The first thing Emily noticed about the Mission was how flat the neighborhood was compared with the steep hill her family lived on. Walking down a sidewalk pocked with blackened chewing gum, they passed buildings with colorful storefronts at street level and bland apartments on the second and third stories above. Emily's dad tilted his nose as they approached a taco bar. Emily could smell the scent of roasting pork.

"Mmm," her dad said. "Maybe we should get lunch here."

Emily steered her dad straight. "Focus."

One lone palm stood out among the leafy shade trees that lined the sidewalk along with parking meters and lampposts. The palm tree marked the corner of Balmy Street, which felt more like an alley than a street, with backyard fences and garage doors butting up to it. Almost every vertical space was painted over in elaborate murals. Bricks were laid in a stripe down the middle of the road, like a red carpet stretching from one end of the block to the other. People wandered up and down with cameras at the ready. A tour guide was speaking to a small group at the opposite end of the block.

Emily's mom adjusted the lens on her camera and began taking photos, focusing on a fence painted with a picture of a group of women holding up their fists in front of a mountain range. Emily's dad pulled out the small notepad and pen he kept in his back pocket and started writing.

"Where is the book supposed to be?" Matthew asked.

"The book?" Emily said, studying the buildings around them. It was hard to tell from the back sides if any of these houses was a Victorian.

"The reason we're here?" Matthew said. "Remember Book Scavenger? The game you obsess over?"

Emily flushed. She'd been so busy thinking about the golden ticket that she'd forgotten she had led her family to think this was a regular book hunt.

"I don't *obsess* over it," she said. "And you don't have to pretend to be interested. Just text your friends or listen to Flush's new album or whatever."

Matthew frowned and flipped his sweatshirt hood over his head, then walked to inspect a mural a few garages down. Boy, did Emily feel like a jerk. Her brother didn't deserve any of that. She wasn't even mad at him. She was supposed to be this Book Scavenger whiz, but she couldn't even solve a simple entry puzzle. And now she was a crummy sister, too.

She went after her brother, who was now standing in front of a mural that showed the character Max from *Where the Wild Things Are* sailing in a boat.

"Hey, we found that book once playing Book Scavenger," Emily said. "It was a long time ago—you probably don't remember."

"Of course I do," Matthew said. "We were in Mitchell, South Dakota. It was the same day we visited the Corn

Palace. The book was hidden by that giant smiling corn sculpture."

"That's right," Emily said. "And we passed those enormous tractors on the drive there, remember? They were as big as a three-story house."

Matthew nodded. "From far away they looked like giant mutant bugs crawling down the road."

They studied Max in his boat for a bit longer; then Emily asked, "Do any of these houses look like they'd be a Victorian to you?"

"A what?" Matthew asked.

"You know, like those famous San Francisco houses that were in the old TV show Mom and Dad made us watch before we moved out here?"

"*Full House?* Oh yeah, I know the type of house you're talking about."

They eyed the buildings up and down Balmy Street. Matthew turned in nearly a full circle until he stopped, facing the next mural over.

"Did you say you were looking for a Victori*AN* or a Victori*ON?*" Matthew asked.

"Victori—" The mural her brother was looking at was of an enormous robot, made up of San Francisco buildings, stomping through a neighborhood. There were all sorts of crazy things around the robot, like a flying cable car, a giant yellow bunny, a car with feet, and a guy on a skateboard holding a scared dog. It was a lot to take in. Matthew kicked his foot forward to underline the name of the mural with the toe of his sneaker: *Victorion.*

"Victorion!" Emily exclaimed. She wasn't supposed to find a house; she was supposed to find a mural. She must have read the clue too fast and missed the odd spelling. Emily hadn't written the clue down because it had seemed simple enough to remember. But this was clearly what she was after.

Now the question was, how would you hide a book on a mural? She scanned up and down the painting, then spotted a colorful crumpled plastic bag tucked between a telephone pole and the mural. Emily pulled the bag free and flattened it against the wall. It was an empty, book-sized bag with a front painted to match a portion of the mural.

Studying the mural like a jigsaw puzzle, she finally spotted the matching location down low. A book inside that empty bag propped in that spot would have blended in with the painting. A small card was taped to the wall:

> # TOO SLOW!
> ## THIS BOOK HAS
> ## BEEN FOUND BY:
> # GLADYSGATSBY14

"Nuts," Emily said in a defeated voice.

"Someone poached it?" Matthew asked. *Poaching* was the Book Scavenger term for when another player located a book first that you had declared on the website. He clamped a hand on her shoulder. "Don't worry. Plenty more books in the sea."

Plenty more books, maybe, but only a few chances left to get into Unlock the Rock.

CHAPTER 6

ON SUNDAY NIGHT Emily tortured herself by stalking the forums and reading all the celebratory, excited posts of the users who'd already qualified for Unlock the Rock. And that was only a fraction of who'd be going— plenty of people didn't post in the forums or even use the website very much at all, like Nisha, who had decided to face her fears and go to the event. Of course she'd had absolutely no problem solving her entry puzzle.

Emily had a notification in her Book Scavenger account—a user named MaddyValentina, who lived in Georgia, had tagged her in a forum post. MaddyValentina had uploaded a scan of a newspaper article and written, *Surly Wombat, you're in our local paper for a series about kids doing amazing things!*

The article recounted Emily and James's adventure with a historical cipher called the unbreakable code. It didn't actually surprise Emily to see this—there had been other newspaper articles, too. More than anything, the clipping reminded her of a fight she and her brother had recently had.

Weeks ago, their dad had taped an article from the local paper to the fridge. That same day Matthew had come home early from hanging out with his friends and scanned the article while getting a snack. He'd said that the reporting was shoddy because he'd been left out of the story. Emily joked back, "Yeah, because watching Flush videos all day long was such critical help."

But Matthew didn't find that funny.

"Are you serious?" he said. "Who helped you with the black light?"

"Are *you* serious?" Emily retorted. "You didn't even want to be there, Matthew."

Before the argument could go further, their mom pulled the clipping off and handed it to Emily to keep in her room. "Enough," she'd said.

That fight had stung extra because Emily and her brother had been in such a good place before then, and she didn't know where his snark had come from.

Now Emily scanned the conversation in the forum thread about what MaddyValentina had posted. Most of the comments were positive and said things like *cool!* and *Surly Wombat is famous!* One person pointed out that Emily was the same Book Scavenger player who'd solved Mr. Griswold's *Gold-Bug* mystery, and then someone asked, *Is Surly Wombat going to Unlock the Rock? Her profile says she's in San Francisco.* The next user said, *I want to be on her team!* and a couple of other Book Scavenger players wrote things along the lines of *That would be so fun!*

It was weird to read the chain because (1) Emily didn't know any of these Book Scavenger users—she recognized a few usernames because they posted frequently in the forums, but that was it—and (2) she'd spent years feeling pretty much invisible and like she had no friends until she met James, and now here were all these people who thought she was great. It would have been nice to have known them back when she'd lived in New Mexico and Colorado and regularly eaten lunch at school by herself.

The positive comments were nice to read, but the words built Surly Wombat into someone who sounded smarter and more clever and all around more awesome than Emily actually felt. But then she read comments from Bookacuda, which made her appreciate that inflated image of herself. He had written, *Why are you all making such a big deal about Swamp Bat? No offense, but it sounds like her friend solved it, not her. And with the Gold-Bug, I'm not impressed. Anyone can win a game if they're the only one playing.*

No offense? Whenever someone started a sentence with *no offense*, you could pretty much count on whatever followed to be offensive. How about, *No offense but you're a jerk, Bookacuda*? Emily didn't actually write that, of course. She didn't comment on the thread at all. There were already several users jumping on Bookacuda for being rude and calling her names. One person simply wrote, *Jealous.*

Emily closed her laptop. Well, Bookacuda and the others didn't need to waste their time deliberating over her, because she probably wasn't going to make it into Unlock the Rock anyway.

All through school on Monday, Emily's brain was a jumble of spiders and clocks and party hats. She knew there must be a trick she was missing for her puzzle, if only she could see it.

Last night, after she couldn't fall asleep, she'd looked again at the map for golden tickets. The one hidden at Grace Cathedral still hadn't been found. She had stayed up late working out the puzzle for that clue, which hadn't been as difficult as she'd thought it would be. The clue said, *Quiet your mind and look east.* Her family had toured Grace Cathedral before, so she knew there were two labyrinths that people walked for meditation. Her guess was that the clue referred to one of those.

That afternoon, Emily spun the combination on her locker and popped open the door to switch out books. A piece of paper fluttered to the floor. Glued to the page were letters cut out from magazines that formed the message:

IF YOU UNLOCK THE ROCK YOU'LL BE SORRY

Emily blinked at the paper, trying to comprehend what she was reading. James's voice greeted her from the other side of her locker door. She wasn't sure why, but her knee-jerk reaction was to hide the note. Before she could stuff it between her books, James said, "You got one, too?"

"Too? You got one?"

James nodded. "Someone doesn't want us to compete."

"Why?"

James shot Emily a *you can't be serious* look. "Maybe because we tracked down a hundred-fifty-year-old lost manuscript and cracked the unbreakable code? We're kind of a threat. At least other people think so."

She could see how knowing Mr. Griswold the way they did and their well-known successes with puzzles and ciphers could make it look like they had an advantage, but Emily had yet to scrape past her entry puzzle, and if and when she managed that, she still had no idea what to expect at the actual event. She was as clueless as anyone else going into Unlock the Rock.

"Should we be worried about this?" she asked, scanning the anonymous message again.

James shrugged. "I wouldn't be surprised if it was

from Maddie. I wouldn't put it past her to do something like this."

"Ouch. I thought she was our friend now."

"She is, but she's still Maddie, and Maddie likes to win. She'd shrug it off as a joke if anyone found out."

Emily crumpled up the paper but then thought better of tossing it in the trash. She straightened it out and slid it into her backpack, just in case she wanted to show it to someone later.

When Emily and James entered their social studies class, Mr. Quisling greeted them with "Two more days!"

"You're going to Unlock the Rock, too?" James asked.

It had taken Emily quite by surprise when she had first learned Mr. Quisling played Book Scavenger. He was a rigid, no-nonsense teacher who stuck to his lectures and lesson plans and was a tough grader. Even his clothes were serious—bland collared shirts, always ironed and tucked in—so there wasn't anything about him that screamed *fun* or *book-hunting adventurer.*

"Miss Linden and I will both be there," Mr. Quisling replied.

Emily and James had befriended Miss Linden, a research librarian for the San Francisco Public Library, when they were trying to solve the unbreakable code. They'd inadvertently brought the two bookish, puzzle-loving adventurers together.

"Oooooh." Maddie's voice spoke up from behind Emily and James. "How romantic."

Seeing Maddie for the first time since finding that note in her locker, Emily couldn't help scrutinizing their friend, like she might find some telltale sign that she had been the one to leave it.

"What?" Maddie said, noticing the extra attention. "Is something on me?"

"No." Emily quickly shook her head. "Just daydreaming."

As she took her seat, James sat next to Emily and said, "Mr. Quisling and Miss Linden are the duo everyone should be worried about. Not you and me."

Their teacher and his girlfriend were the true team to beat—Emily agreed with that. Regardless, whoever was trying to scare her and James didn't have to go to such extremes.

Emily was doing a bang-up job on her own of keeping herself out of the game.

CHAPTER 7

UNTIL ERROL ROY stepped through the main entry of the Bayside Press office building on Monday morning, it hadn't occurred to him that Garrison Griswold might not be in. He hadn't called ahead or made an appointment, because he knew it was entirely possible, if Griswold was the sort to hold a grudge, that he might not be willing to hear Errol out. It seemed like the element of surprise could work in Errol's favor. It also allowed him the option of changing his mind at the last second about setting his plan in action.

As Errol rode the elevator up to the sixth floor, he thought about the one and only time he'd seen Garrison Griswold in person. It was decades ago, before Griswold started Bayside Press. Griswold had written Roy a letter praising his writing and invited him to do an event at the bookstore he co-owned.

Errol had a budding career at the time, although he never would have used that word, *career*. He'd simply been amazed he could string together enough sentences to tell a story anyone would want to publish, let alone to be able to do it more than once. He had ignored Griswold's letter, but the man persisted. They finally spoke on the phone, and Errol told him he'd never done public events before and was uncomfortable with them. He didn't want to talk to strangers about his books. He was interested in the writing, not the attention.

They'd keep it simple, Griswold said. Low-key. He told Errol about the impact his books—the three he'd published at that time—had had on his customers. That was a revelation: Errol Roy's stories lived on in other people. When he was writing, Errol lived each scene in his imagination, but when the book was done, that was it for him. He moved on from the story and recalled the characters and events the way you do distant memories or people you once knew. But the idea that a past experience for him could be a *present* experience for someone else, intercepting that reader's life, sometimes in a meaningful way . . . None of that had occurred to Errol until his phone conversation with Garrison Griswold.

So he'd agreed to show up at the bookstore and meet some of those readers. What harm could it do? How difficult could it be?

When Errol arrived on the agreed-upon day, he saw rows of folding chairs and a podium and people milling about. Balloons clustered in front of bookshelves, and a handmade banner read WELCOME ERROL ROY! There were cameras.

This was as low-key and simple as the Transamerica building was square.

Errol had realized immediately that he'd made a mistake. He shouldn't have agreed to this. The hum of people flooded his ears, and he was drowning in the noise until a young man waved in front of his face to grab his attention.

"Welcome!" the man said. "Sit anywhere you'd like."

The word *sit* was tossed over his head like a life preserver. He knew the man was Hollister, the co-owner. Roy had been a customer in the store many times before—though he'd never introduced himself. There was nothing about Errol that screamed *author*, and this was a few decades before the Internet. There was no photo on Errol Roy's book jackets, per his request. He blended in with most of the other men idling around the bookstore that day—a middle-aged guy with a thick beard and mustache. Nonetheless, it was a surprise to realize that Hollister didn't recognize him.

He was anonymous.

Hollister gestured to a folding chair, and this was the moment Errol could have—should have—said he was the author, but instead he sat. What would happen, he wondered, if he remained seated and didn't volunteer who he was?

Minutes passed.

A tall, slender man with curly hair hurried to

Hollister's side, and they held a hushed conversation that involved multiple glances at their watches and then through the large picture window to the street. Errol knew this man was Griswold.

Garrison Griswold edged toward the front of the mostly seated crowd. It shamed Errol that he couldn't find it within himself to move, to stand up. Even if only to leave. He was frozen to his chair, waiting to see what would happen. Waiting to see if someone was going to point at him and cry out, "There he is! Imposter!"

Griswold stepped to the podium, and Errol expected him to open with an apology, explain that Errol Roy hadn't shown up, and tell everyone to go home. Instead Griswold said in a cheery, theatrical tone, "Greetings, book lovers!"

People on either side of Errol smiled and murmured replies. Errol watched, stunned and a little impressed, as Griswold spoke about Errol Roy's latest book and got the crowd involved in a discussion on what made a good mystery. If Errol hadn't already known he'd stood up his own event, he never would have guessed Griswold was in a tough spot.

At one point a young man raised his hand and hesitantly asked, "I thought the author was going to be here?" He sounded embarrassed to have assumed such a thing.

"Ah, yes." Griswold nodded and looked down to collect his thoughts before gesturing to the hanging banner. "We did invite him, and we hoped Errol Roy would come, but I'm sorry to say it doesn't look like he will make it."

The audience groaned. Errol looked at his neighbors with muted surprise.

"I know!" Griswold nodded his agreement with their groans. "I'm disappointed, too. I admire his writing greatly, and it would be wonderful to hear from the man himself. But!" Griswold held up his index finger. "I have something fun in store for you all."

And then, to make an unexpected day even more so, Griswold led everyone in a parlor game called Murder in the Dark, adapting the players so they were characters from Roy's latest novel. What Garrison Griswold understood and honored was that everyone had gathered in that space because they loved books and wanted to be entertained or connect with other book people.

Errol Roy didn't know it then, but that incident had set him firmly on the path he would take forward as a well-known—and well-known for being highly reclusive—author. It hadn't occurred to him until just now, recollecting that day as he rode the elevator up to the Bayside Press offices, that it was entirely possible the experience had been a similar turning point for Garrison Griswold, setting him on the path he would take forward as well.

The elevator dinged its arrival at the Bayside Press floor. The doors opened to a receptionist desk in a room garishly decorated in burgundy and blue everything. Errol Roy approached the kid, who looked to be in his twenties, sitting behind the desk, scrolling through photos on his phone. "Is Garrison Griswold in today?" he asked.

"Do you have an appointment?" the kid asked, not looking up.

"Is he in?"

Keeping his head angled to his phone, the kid rolled his eyes up to look at Errol. "I'm a temp, but I'm pretty sure you need an appointment."

"Could you tell him Errol Roy would like to speak with him?"

The temp's mouth parted. "No, you're not," he finally said. "You are not him."

"I am." Errol pulled his wallet from his pocket and slid out his photo ID.

"No way! Is this for real? I didn't think you existed."

Errol Roy wasn't sure how his books could exist if he didn't until the kid explained. "I thought there were like ghostwriters or something. Wait." He narrowed his eyes and then looked over his shoulder and behind the phone on the table. "Is this a hidden-camera show? Are you tricking me?"

"Could you please just let Mr. Griswold know I'm here and I'd like to speak with him?"

"Oh yes! Of course." The temp lifted the phone and pressed a button, then spoke to someone on the other end.

". . . He showed me his ID and everything. . . . I don't

know why he's here." The temp covered the mouthpiece and leaned forward. "What did you want to talk to Mr. Griswold about?"

"Unlock the Rock," Errol replied.

The kid raised his eyebrows and relayed Errol's answer. Finally he hung up the phone and said, "His assistant will be out in a minute to lead you back."

While Errol Roy waited, the temp peppered him with questions about his best-known book, which had been made into an award-winning movie almost two decades ago. That movie had become a cult classic, which was how someone who was probably a toddler when it was made would be familiar with it.

"Did you meet Clint Eastwood? And that rumor about you having a cameo—was that true? I always thought you were the bus driver, but now that I'm seeing you in person, I don't think so anymore. Unless you wore a lot of makeup?"

The kid kept talking even though Errol didn't answer any of his questions. That was something Errol had learned a long time ago about being quiet. Sometimes the more you stayed silent, the more the other person would blab.

He hadn't met Clint Eastwood or had a cameo or even set foot on the movie set. He'd never even seen the movie. The truth was that that particular book was the only one of his that he couldn't stand, and he did every-thing possible not to think about it. He'd sold the movie rights because he needed the money back then, and he hadn't expected it to blow up into a cultural phenomenon or realized how uncomfortable he would be having that particular novel widely known and celebrated. He'd been haunted by a ghost of his own creation ever since, presented to him now in the form of this twenty-something temp who wouldn't stop talking.

"Mr. Roy?" a chipper voice behind him said, and Errol turned with relief to find a man wearing a burgundy and blue plaid vest.

"I'm Jack, Mr. Griswold's assistant." Jack extended his hand. "It's a pleasure to meet you."

"You match this room," Errol replied.

"Bayside Press colors," Jack said. "Not a requirement of working here—I'm just having fun with it. Follow me."

Errol Roy followed Jack down a hallway lined with paintings of famous San Francisco authors in ludicrous costumes. He couldn't help smirking when he saw his own: Errol Roy as a mummy. Clever way to portray him when nobody knew what he looked like.

Garrison Griswold was already standing when they entered his office. "Wonderful to finally meet you after all these years," Griswold said.

Errol couldn't tell if that was a barb buried in his welcome. "You too," he replied.

Garrison Griswold stared at him intensely, like he was trying to memorize every detail. It was unnerving, so Errol focused on the Rube Goldberg machine in the office instead. It was a large glass case that enclosed what looked like a miniature roller coaster for marbles, made out of levers and slides and sprockets and rotating wheels and the like.

"Thank you for taking the time to speak with me," Errol said to the marble that *clack-clack-clacked* down a miniature staircase.

"Of course. Come, let's have a seat."

"I'm fine standing. I won't take up much of your time."

Errol glanced away from the machine and realized that Griswold and Jack had already sat down in the sitting area of the office. Errol perched on the edge of an armchair. He wanted to get this over with, so his words came out in one long rush.

"I'd like to participate in Unlock the Rock—or, rather, help craft the narrative of the game—and I have an idea for how I could insert my own mystery into whatever you've already planned, assuming you don't mind making a few changes. My only request is that the story I craft for the game remain a surprise—for everyone, including you."

Griswold nodded thoughtfully. "Were you thinking of writing something up or—"

Errol cut him off. "It's also important to me that I be there to present my story."

"In person?" Griswold asked, surprised.

"Yes, on Alcatraz, as myself at the event."

Griswold and Jack exchanged a look.

"Don't get me wrong," Griswold began. "I know I

speak for Hollister as well when I say we greatly appreciate your gesture, but I have to ask: Why? Why now?"

Errol had anticipated this question. Concentrating on the lamp next to Griswold, he carefully stated his answer. "I'm getting on in years, and I've told all the stories I'm interested in telling, except for one. Unlock the Rock would offer me a unique way to tell that story, and I'm not sure I'll have another opportunity." For the last bit of what he wanted to say, Errol risked looking directly at Garrison Griswold. "I would also hope that in participating, I might be making amends for having disappointed people in the past."

Now it was Mr. Griswold's turn to avert his eyes. He smiled lightly and said, "I appreciate that, but no amends are necessary. Your help, however, would be tremendous."

Errol Roy nodded, to acknowledge Mr. Griswold's offer of forgiveness.

"And, of course, you'll have to cooperate with Alcatraz's guidelines for events on their premises, and you and I will have to draw up an official agreement."

"None of that will be a problem," Errol replied.

"Having an author of your stature involved with Unlock the Rock would bring a lot of additional attention to it and to the bookstore's reopening . . . ," Mr. Griswold said tentatively.

"Yes," Errol agreed. "And I'm fine with you publicizing that I will be involved, if that is helpful to you. As long as I am the only one who will know the details of my story."

Mr. Griswold leaned forward, his eyes creased with concern. "But you've cultivated a very private life, and doing this might change things for you. Are you sure you're okay with that?"

No, I'm not sure, Errol thought, but what he said was, "Yes."

CHAPTER 8

AFTER SCHOOL, Emily and James walked home, but she was only half listening as her friend talked. All she could think about was what she would do if she couldn't solve her entry puzzle for Unlock the Rock. She could explain not going by faking being sick, but that wouldn't solve anything—she'd still miss out, and she didn't want that. Maybe she could pretend to have lost her ticket? Would they let her play the game then? It was probably a simple thing for Mr. Griswold or Jack to review the website to check if Surly Wombat had qualified before replacing her ticket.

They walked their usual route home past Hollister's bookstore. They used to stop in and say hello most afternoons, but they hadn't been able to for more than a month, since the fire that had ravaged his shop had forced him to close temporarily. The community had rallied around him, as evidenced by the store window papered over with posters, cards, and sheets of butcher paper covered in different handwriting in various colors of marker. Customers and neighbors had let him know how much he and his shop were valued with notes of support like: *You'll be back, better than ever!*

Parked in front of the store was an old VW bus that a neighbor had donated to Hollister so he could have a mobile bookstore while the actual store was under repair. Another neighbor had painted the vehicle with a sign that said HOLLISTER'S BOOK BUS. Often Hollister or his new employee, Diego, would be spotted driving it around to deliver book orders, or parked at a food-truck night. Sometimes Emily could hear the bus traveling through the neighborhood from blocks away, because Hollister liked to play the song "There Should Be a Book" by Lee Dorsey over a loudspeaker.

Emily kept thinking about her predicament as James pressed his hands to the window of the bookstore to peer through a gap in the notes and cards. "I see Diego unpacking boxes of books," he said. "No sign of Hollister."

Emily was looking at a drawing a child had made. It looked like a person riding a train made of books, with hearts coming out of the smokestack. In beginner hand-writing, the note said, *Books are my ticket to other worlds.*

Suddenly Emily knew what she had to do.

"I forgot something at school!" she blurted out.

James looked at her like she had hiccupped bubbles. "What did you forget?"

"My . . . math textbook. Go ahead without me so your grandma doesn't wonder where you are."

Before James could say anything else, Emily spun around and ran back the way they'd come. Their school was in the opposite direction from where she wanted to go, but she had to wait until she knew she was out of view of James before she turned down a side street and headed instead toward Grace Cathedral.

The cathedral was an immense Gothic-style building that took up an entire block and was built higher than street level, so there was a long and wide set of stairs leading up to it. In front of the entrance and off to the side, opposite a courtyard, was a small alcove where the first labyrinth was laid out on the ground. Cement benches and planters filled with shrubs and trees created a border around the labyrinth.

When Emily had moved to San Francisco last fall and heard about the labyrinths, she'd imagined they would be more like mazes with high walls and twisty turns and dead ends. But each of the labyrinths at Grace Cathedral was flat, made out of stones placed in a pattern to form a large circle with a serpentine path inside that curved back and forth around itself until it reached a flower-shaped center.

Although Emily could cross the flat labyrinth and go directly to the center, she didn't. It felt disrespectful to not walk the path, especially as this was on the property of the cathedral.

She entered the labyrinth and stepped heel-toe,

heel-toe as quickly as possible, but a funny thing happened as she made her way to the middle. The things she was worried about—not finding the golden ticket, not making it into Unlock the Rock, who had left her that note—loosened with every heel-toe step, until one by one they broke free and she was left simply concentrating on her goal.

When she reached the flower, she faced east to the park across the street. Emily closed her eyes and took a deep breath in. She exhaled and opened her eyes. Looking forward, she saw nothing unusual. Nothing

under or on the benches. The planter looked like your average . . .

An odd patch of ivy stood out.

It was a different green from the other plants and had a slight sheen—the more she stared, the more certain Emily became that it wasn't real. She was certain she'd found the hiding place for the book that held the golden ticket and was about to dart forward when she heard a young voice shout, "Papa, we're almost there! I can see the top of the stairs!"

Between the trees that separated the labyrinth and the long set of stairs that led up to the cathedral, Emily soon saw a cap, worn by an old man, bobbing up the steps. The cap stopped moving for a second, and Emily could hear a man's voice say, "Hold on, Iris. Give me a second."

"We're going to find it—I just know it!" The little girl, who had to be Iris, bounced on the stairs, so her head was visible, and then not, visible, then not.

"Don't get your hopes up yet, dear. Let's wait and see what we see."

Realizing this young girl and her grandfather were obviously looking for the golden ticket, too, made Emily's shoulders droop. All she had to do was run forward and grab it and it would be hers. But watching that girl's braids flap up and down with every bounce, Emily remembered being about the same age, when she was in third grade and new to Book Scavenger and so excited to go on book hunts, and so *crushed* when the book she'd been scouting wasn't there. Not that she didn't get excited now, but it was a different feeling when it was all brand-new. Emily knew this golden ticket was one of very few left, and if Iris was also looking for it, then it might be the young girl's only chance to get into Unlock the Rock.

Emily looked from the fake clump of ivy to the stairs where Iris and her grandfather stood, and back to the ivy.

She took a deep breath, spun on one foot, and walked away.

CHAPTER 9

SURPRISINGLY, EMILY felt okay about leaving the golden ticket behind. She knew Iris was going to be ecstatic when she found it, and Emily did still have one more try with her puzzle. If she got the answer wrong again, well, that was just a chance she was going to take. There had to be a trick to solving it, like the fake ivy hiding the book near the labyrinth. Once you saw it, you couldn't unsee it.

But first you had to see it.

When Emily turned onto her street, James was on the sidewalk in front of their building, a device in his hands to direct the remote control car he'd made. The car whirred up the very steep hill toward Emily until it tipped over on its back. She scooped it up and righted the vehicle, facing it downhill, then scuttled alongside the car as James drove it back to himself.

"Did you get it?" he asked when she stopped in front of the building.

Emily froze. How had James known she'd gone to look for a golden ticket?

He gave her that hiccupping-bubbles look again. "Your math book?" he reminded her.

"Oh. Yeah, I did."

James's dark brown eyes reflected such genuine concern, she couldn't keep the truth from him any longer. She had to come clean.

"Actually . . . I didn't forget a book. I was trying to find a golden ticket."

"You *were*? Did you . . . ." James looked to either side of them, even though nobody else was outside, and lowered his voice. "Did you not get in?"

"No—I mean, I don't know. I have one try left. I've been kind of freaking out. The pressure, you know?"

"Why didn't you tell me? I would have gone with you."

"I know," Emily said. "I just feel dumb that I'm stuck on a puzzle."

James shrugged. "Everyone gets stuck sometimes. If it wasn't a challenge, it wouldn't be fun. I can try and help you."

Emily shook her head firmly, her ponytail wagging. "Thanks, but no. I need to solve it myself."

Emily opened the Unlock the Rock entry page, determined to click "yes" this time and give her puzzle one last go, when a knock on her open door startled her.

Emily's mom stood in the hallway. "Almost time to go!"

"Go where?" Emily asked, exasperated.

Her mom pressed her hands to her hips and mirrored her exasperated look. "Emily! First you make fun of my favorite book, which I beg you to read, and now you forget about the author talk?!"

"Right, right," Emily muttered, closing her laptop. "Lacey Lopez."

"It's Lucy Leonard. Even if you're not excited about her, you can be excited about supporting Hollister. He's the one who'll be asking her questions tonight. Surely that's something you can look forward to."

It was putting off the inevitable, but Emily was a little relieved she wasn't going to find out her Unlock the Rock fate quite yet.

In the past when her family had gone to hear authors talk about their new books, it was always in a bookstore—one of the various stores here in San Francisco or where they'd lived in previous states—but tonight's event was being held in a theater. Emily's parents had said it would be a small theater, but it didn't seem small to Emily. There were several hundred seats above and below them.

They sat in red velvet chairs in the balcony. The ceiling was an elaborate pattern of paneled stars with chandeliers hanging down. Below, the stage was spare, decorated only with a rug, two armchairs, and an end table in between.

Matthew whistled, taking in the space. "This lady must be a big deal."

"Her book is excellent." Their mother nudged Emily with her elbow. "It's not too late to read *The Twain Conspiracy*." She was a Superfan, with a capital *S*, and had kept trying to get Emily to read the book since the unbreakable code had had to do with Mark Twain. Her mom said the book was a page-turner, but Emily hadn't been able to get into it.

"Does it have a psychic in it?" Emily didn't have high hopes that an author who wrote something she had found boring would be very interesting to listen to, so she'd brought the book she was in the middle of, *Hello, Universe*, as well as her flashlight pen so she could read and even make notes in the dark. Sometimes when Emily read books, she liked to write comments or thoughts in the margins. It was something she'd been doing as long as she'd been reading on her own.

"I can't say I remember a psychic," her mom said.

"Well, *this* book has a psychic."

Emily's dad leaned forward in his seat, peering down at all the people settling into the rows below. "Your mom's not the only one crazy about this book. Look at everyone here!"

"Just because something is liked by *some* of the

people doesn't mean it needs to be liked by *all* of the people," Emily countered. "Plenty of people love macaroni and cheese, but Matthew hates it."

Matthew made a retching noise. "Ugh. Even the thought of it is gross."

Emily's mom smiled. "Point taken. It's good to stretch yourself sometimes, though."

Emily held up *Hello, Universe.* "Maybe you should stretch yourself and read this."

"You're right! Maybe I should."

"Shhh." Emily's dad nodded to the stage. "Here comes Hollister."

The chandeliers dimmed. The bookseller looked so small as he shuffled to the center of the stage. He wore his button-down shirt untucked, and it billowed as he walked, his graying dreads gathered loosely behind him. The event had been scheduled by Hollister's bookstore before it suffered the fire, and Emily knew he'd been looking forward to it. He'd been the one to tell her mom about it when she bought her copy of the book from him. With everything Hollister had lost in the fire, Emily was glad that tonight couldn't be taken from him.

Matthew cupped his hands around his mouth and yelled, "Yeah, Hollister!" then leaned to their dad and asked, "Am I allowed to do that in a fancy place like this?" Before he'd finished his question, more people called Hollister's name and started applauding.

Even though he was far away, Emily could tell

Hollister was surprised. Or maybe embarrassed. He batted their cheers away, which only amped up the volume.

"What a way to start the night," he said.

People jumped to their feet, giving him a standing ovation.

Hollister shook his head and turned away from the crowd for a moment before facing them again and saying, "Come on now, people. I need to hold it together for Lucy Leonard. Help me out here."

Everyone laughed and settled back into their seats.

"Seriously, though, thank you, each and every one of you, for your support for Hollister's. I imagine you've heard about Unlock the Rock, Garrison Griswold's latest challenge. That was going to be a fund-raiser for my store, but you all—my neighborhood, the bookseller community, strangers—came through for me in ways I never would have expected or dreamed. So now we're calling it a *fun*-raiser, and I hope to see many of you there to raise the *fun*, all right?"

With the cheering and hooting that followed, it felt to Emily like the whole *theater* must be going to Unlock the Rock. She slouched in her seat and doodled a spider, a clock, and a party hat in the margin of the page she'd left off on in *Hello, Universe*.

Hollister continued, "If I don't see you there, we'll be raising the fun again at the grand reopening of my store Sunday. Can you believe that? Thanks to our community rallying, Hollister's bookstore will be open again next week."

Now, that was applause that Emily was happy to join in on. People started to stand again in waves, but Hollister wagged his hands for them to sit. When the noise died down enough for people to hear, he said, "Let's not start *that* up again," and everyone laughed.

Hollister introduced Lucy Leonard, and the woman walked out onstage. Her glossy, dark hair hung like one smooth sheet to her shoulders, and thick, red-framed glasses stood out against her pale skin.

Emily's mom shook her head reverentially and said, "Amazing that someone that young can write books as well as she does."

"She doesn't look young—she looks your age," Emily whispered back.

Her mom bumped her shoulder to Emily's. "Hush up," she said. She leaned forward to concentrate as Hollister and the author settled into the chairs.

"I have to tell you," Lucy Leonard said to the audience. "If I wasn't already on deadline for a different book, *this* is the story I'd want to write. The bookseller as a hero." She gestured widely to the crowd, then turned to Hollister. "Your community wouldn't have done what they did for you if you hadn't been faithfully serving them all these years and made genuine connections with your customers."

Hollister shooed her compliments away with the

sheet of paper he held in his hand with notes for his interview. "Enough about me already. I want to jump on something you just said—you're on deadline for another book? Can you tell us about it?"

"Well . . ." Lucy Leonard looked around the theater. "What I *can* say is that my next book is about Harriet Beecher Stowe. She was Mark Twain's neighbor when he lived in Hartford, Connecticut, so I was led quite naturally to her through my research for *The Twain Conspiracy*. I almost felt like Twain himself led me down the path to write this book."

Hollister cocked his head. "Really? How is that?"

The author pursed her lips in a secretive smile. "Let's say I found something in a collection of his letters that planted the seed for what my focus would be."

"Interesting . . ." Hollister dragged out the word.

"More than anything, I chose Stowe because she was a fascinating person. Mother of seven, a prolific writer, author of *Uncle Tom's Cabin*, the antislavery novel published in 1852 that helped fuel the abolitionist movement. Her words connected with readers in that pre–Civil War atmosphere and the book took off. *Uncle Tom's Cabin* sold more books than any other book in the nineteenth century, second only to the Bible. Now, I've been very fortunate to have *The Twain Conspiracy* on the bestseller list for twenty-six weeks, but that's nothing compared to having published one of the most popular books of an entire century."

Despite Emily's reluctance to be here and lack of interest in Lucy Leonard's book, she found herself holding *Hello, Universe* open-side down in her lap and listening instead to what the author was saying.

"And Stowe got this recognition in a time when women didn't have the right to vote, and female writers often weren't taken seriously. It wasn't uncommon for women to sign their work 'anonymous' or use a male pen name—as was the case with George Eliot, who wrote *Middlemarch*—in order for their words to be valued and respected. So for Harriet Beecher Stowe to break through those barriers, and to be invited on speaking tours in our country and abroad in Europe, was exceptional."

Hollister nodded along as Lucy Leonard spoke. "I look forward to reading that. You mentioned *The Twain Conspiracy*'s continuing run on the bestseller list, and of course it was also a National Book Award finalist—how does it feel to follow in your own footsteps after writing a book that was so warmly received?"

"I try not to think about it that way," Lucy Leonard said. "I focus on the task at hand and the aspects of Harriet Beecher Stowe's life that I'm interested in, and the best way, narratively, to bring that to readers. But I'll be honest. . . ." Lucy turned to the audience, her head angled up so Emily could almost imagine she'd singled her out of the crowd and was speaking directly to her. "The expectations do get to me sometimes. You just have to go for it."

Hollister continued the conversation, but all Emily could think about was what the author had just said. All that pressure Emily felt to get into Unlock the Rock, the expectations from others based off her previous Book Scavenger triumphs, the expectations *she* had for herself . . . The lady's Mark Twain book might not have hooked Emily, but she couldn't let go of Lucy Leonard's words: *You just have to go for it.*

THAT NIGHT, when the Cranes got back to their apartment, Emily marched straight to her laptop, logged into the Book Scavenger website, and opened the entry puzzle for the final time. Whatever the outcome might be, she was going for it.

$$\text{🕷} + \text{🕷} + \text{🕷} = 24$$

$$\text{🕷} - \text{🕐} = 5$$

$$\text{🕐} + \text{🕐} + \text{🎉} = 10$$

$$\text{🕐} + \text{🎉} \times \text{🕷} = \text{?}$$

"Okay, you can do this," Emily muttered.

The spiders *had* to be equal to eight because eight plus eight plus eight equaled twenty-four. There was no other possibility. And then eight minus three equaled five, so the clock was three. Then three plus three plus four would be ten. . . .

Emily was starting to feel despair creeping in again. This was exactly what she'd done before, and she already knew that wasn't right. She closed her eyes, took a deep breath, and thought, *Just go for it*.

She opened her eyes and looked at the fourth line. It started with a clock, so that would be equal to three. . . .

"Wait." The clock on the fourth line was set to four o'clock. She double-checked the other clocks. They were set to three o'clock!

"That's the trick!" she whispered.

The spider was equal to eight, and a spider had *eight* legs.

The clock in lines two and three were each equal to three, and they were set to three o'clock.

The party hat in the third line down was equal to four. "Four dots," Emily realized, and the other party hat had *five* dots.

The fourth line wasn't three plus four times eight like she'd first thought. It was four plus five times eight. Following the order of operations meant you did the multiplication first, so five times eight equaled forty, plus four equaled forty-four.

Emily double-checked her math, then typed in the answer and pressed "Enter."

CONGRATULATIONS!

Emily whooped, then flopped back on her bed. She rolled over and grabbed her notebook, ripping a piece of paper free. In her and James's secret code she scribbled:

B CXV BF!
(I got in!)

Emily crossed to her window, pushed up the sash, and dropped the note in the bucket that hung outside. As she tugged on the pulley, the bucket rose to James's window directly above hers. She secured the rope to keep the bucket in place.

She grabbed the broom propped in the corner of her room, which had a split-open tennis ball stuck on top, and used that to knock on her ceiling in the same pattern she and James always used when they had bucket mail: *Thud. Thud-thud-thud. Thud.*

When James's reply was on its way down, he knocked back. She removed the note from the bucket and deciphered his reply:

XI EXLPSU DXL QBQ.
(Of course you did.)

It was nice to have a friend who believed in you more than you believed in yourself.

The next day, Tuesday, Emily and her friends spent their entire lunch period plotting what to bring for the game. At least that was what she and James and Maddie and Nisha talked about. Vivian was getting a head start on her homework, and because Devin hadn't gotten into the event, Kevin had decided not to try out. He didn't want to go if his brother wouldn't be there, so the twins played a card game off to the side.

Very little was known about what Unlock the Rock would actually involve. The only guideline provided was that they could bring one regular-sized backpack each, filled with anything they thought could be useful, as long as it wasn't a weapon or dangerous or alive. Determining what could be useful felt like an impossible task since, as Nisha pointed out, anything could be useful depending on what you were doing.

"I'll bring rubber gloves in case we have to wash dishes!" James said.

"A mousetrap in case we are catching mice," Maddie added.

"I'll pack whipped cream in case we're making sundaes," Emily said.

"One of you should bring a calculator, in case there are equations to solve," Vivian interjected.

"That . . . might actually be useful," James said, and they wrote it down on their list.

After they'd brainstormed a bit more, James said to Emily, "Tell me again—after Mr. Griswold announced Errol Roy would be designing the mystery for us to solve on Alcatraz, what were people saying in the Book Scavenger forums?"

Emily grinned. She'd told James this small bit of gossip on their way to school, not realizing he was going to keep asking to hear it again and again, like a little kid with his favorite picture book.

"The person in the forums said Errol Roy himself came into the Bayside Press building when he asked to be involved in the game."

"I still don't get why that is so exciting," Maddie said. "Garrison Griswold runs a publishing company, Book Scavenger is a game about hiding books. What's so amazing about an author having something to do with one of his games?"

James scoffed, thumping his hand to his chest like he'd swallowed something down the wrong tube.

"An author? *An* author? Is J. K. Rowling just *an* author? Is Tolkien just *an* author? Errol Roy is the greatest mystery writer of all time. He wrote *Liars and Thieves* and *No Witness* and *Rise of the Moon* and a bunch of other classics."

Devin looked up from his game. "I know *Liars and Thieves*. That was a great movie."

"The book was way better," James said. To the rest

he explained, "It's about a private investigator who has this ex-convict come to him who says he's being black-mailed and framed for a robbery. The convict's turned his life around and doesn't want to mess anything up. The PI believes him and starts to investigate and then—" James holds up his hands. "I don't want to ruin it. Just read it. Errol Roy is so well known, the library has an annual Errol Roy Day, where they host a mystery theater based on one of his books. Local celebrities are often in them, like the mayor or a Giants player." He pointed to Emily. "Mr. Griswold participated a few times."

"So you're a megafan," Maddie said, jotting down another item on their brainstorming list. "That's why it's a big deal."

"No," James said. "I mean, yes, but no, that's not why it's a big deal. Errol Roy is super private. Nobody even knows who he is! There are rumors that he's not even real and his books are written by a bunch of differ-ent people."

"Like Carolyn Keene?" Emily asked. "The author of the Nancy Drew series?"

"She's not a real person?" Nisha asked, looking a bit crestfallen. "I didn't know that."

"If Errol Roy really was at Bayside Press the other day, that's the first time *ever* there has been an actual confirmed sighting. He is so mysterious, I didn't even know he lived in this area. And I've read all his books!"

Vivian looked up from her math problems. "But you knew about the Errol Roy mystery-theater thing," she pointed out.

"Well, yeah," James said. "But he was never there. I thought every city had one! Every city should. Maybe they do? Anyway. All I'm saying is if Errol Roy has something to do with Unlock the Rock, it's going to be epic."

CHAPTER 11

ERROL ROY stood in the entry to his apartment. His curtains were drawn. Dash was curled up in the reading chair—his favorite spot—with the lamp glowing on the table beside him. Tomorrow afternoon was Garrison Griswold's event, and there were a few things Errol still needed to set up.

He perched his panama hat on his head, opened the top drawer of the cabinet next to the front door, and removed both his set of keys and the spare. His hands were trembling, which at his eighty-six years of age wasn't abnormal, but these tremors were so bad he couldn't stop the keys from clinking together like sleigh bells.

"Be good, Dash," he whispered before slipping outside his apartment.

He crossed the hall and knocked on Valerie's door.

He wasn't sure he'd ever done that before. She opened it slowly and peered through the gap. "Oh! Ernie, hello." She pushed the door wide. Her sweat suit was ruby red this evening.

"Did your cat get out again?" she asked.

That's right, he *had* knocked on her door once before, years ago, when Dash went missing.

"No, but funny you should mention my cat." Errol focused on her doorbell. "I'll be gone tomorrow afternoon and evening. Could you check in on him? Dash is his name. Give him fresh food and water."

"Of course, of course. I'd be happy to," Valerie said.

Errol extended his spare key but hesitated before releasing it into her palm. There were things he wanted to convey to Valerie, but he didn't know how.

"It's important to me that Dash is well taken care of. He's a great cat."

"Of *course*, dear, of course. I understand—he's your baby. You know, I've had cats most of my life, so I really do understand. I nearly adopted another last year, but at my age it seemed like that would be foolish. Some days I think it was foolish not to. Your Dash will be well taken care of tomorrow—don't worry about that for a second."

Valerie plucked the key from his fingers. Errol remained standing there, feeling like there was more to say but the words weren't coming to him.

"Well," he finally said.

Valerie stared at him curiously but kindly. "It's scary being on our own, isn't it?" she said. "Not having any family. I understand."

She couldn't really. She had a daughter who checked in on her, and a niece in Austin who visited Valerie once a year. Errol only had Dash.

"Yes, well, thank you," Errol finally said. He walked away to the elevator and set out to complete his final and most important task before Unlock the Rock.

CHAPTER 12

ON WEDNESDAY AFTERNOON, Emily and her family walked past the vertical green ALCATRAZ LANDING sign that marked the entrance of Pier 33, and under the blue and burgundy balloon arch that welcomed Unlock the Rock contestants.

Emily could not believe she was actually here. Contestants of all ages swarmed the pier, wearing backpacks and bundled in jackets and knit hats on this gray San Francisco day. An eager energy jolted through the crowd like an electric charge.

The pier was a large swath of asphalt between two long warehouse buildings that jutted over the water. In the distance was a white ferryboat with ALCATRAZ CRUISES written across the top, but nobody was boarding yet. Instead the contestants circled a long bank of cubicles set up in the middle of the pier. Inside each cubicle was an identical pile of gigantic blocks. The blocks were each the size of an end table, and it looked as if there was a different image printed on every side of the cube.

A game setup, Emily figured. She counted ten stalls on the side they faced, and it looked like there was an identical set on the back side.

Emily's dad rested one hand on her shoulder and the other on Matthew's. "I feel better knowing the two of you will be together."

"Two?" Emily looked beyond her parents and her brother to see if her dad had spotted James. Her mom gave Matthew a hug and said, "Have a great time."

"You mean *us* two?" Emily asked. To her brother she said, "You're staying?"

"You didn't know he was doing this?" their dad said.

Their mom pushed Matthew to arm's length so she could see his face. "I thought you told your sister."

Matthew shrugged. "She didn't believe me when I said I'd get in."

Emily's mouth hung open. She had noticed her brother had brought his backpack when they'd left their house, but she'd figured he was going somewhere after their parents dropped her off at the ferry.

"Are your friends here?" Emily asked.

"Nope." Matthew plugged in one earbud and left the other dangling.

"So . . ." Emily watched him swipe, swipe, swipe away song selections until he got to one he liked. "Why are you here, then?"

The look Matthew gave her was a cross between annoyed and hurt. "I'm on the Book Scavenger advisory, too, you know. I care about Hollister's store. Besides, it sounded cool."

"Well, it's good to know you'll have each other around," their dad interjected. "We trust Mr. Griswold and Hollister, of course, and the waiver we signed was reassuring about supervision for kids and teens, but still—"

"They'll also have me," James piped up, having just arrived at the pier himself. "And them." He waved and Emily turned to see their friends standing together in the distance. The lowering sun reflected off Nisha's orange-framed glasses, and Maddie stood a head taller, with her arms crossed as she observed the sifting crowd of players.

"Hey, kids!" they heard a familiar voice call.

"Hollister!" Emily and James ran over to give the bookseller a hug. Without his store being open so they could drop in and visit, it had been several weeks since they'd last been able to talk with their friend. Emily had seen Hollister from a distance at the Lucy Leonard event, but there had been too many people that night to find him and say hi.

"You have a beard now," Matthew noted. "I like it."

"You should name it," James said. "Looks like a Frankie to me."

Hollister laughed and shook his head. "No. No way. If I put a razor to my face, I'd feel like I was in a horror show."

The *dum-dum* of a microphone being tapped drew everyone's attention to the far end of the game setup, where Mr. Griswold stood. He wore what Emily considered his Book Scavenger costume—a burgundy and silver-blue striped suit and top hat with matching walking stick, and a silver bow tie. Emily had seen him dressed like this often in his online videos and photos, but never in person. A little thrill of excitement ran down her spine.

"Greetings, scavengers!" Mr. Griswold welcomed the contestants.

His words charged through the crowd, and everyone erupted into cheers and applause. Emily joined in, feeling so happy to be part of this sea of strangers. It was a mix of young, old, and in between, a range of skin tones and fashion styles. You wouldn't have guessed they had anything in common unless you noticed the Book Scavenger emblem on shirts and hats and pins and one man's tattoo on his calf.

"I better get over there," Hollister said. "Good luck tonight, kids!"

After Hollister left, James said, "Let's go join Nisha and Maddie."

Emily and Matthew hugged their parents once more; then they and James wove through the crowd, their backpacks bumping against people, until they stood next to their friends.

Mr. Griswold waited for everyone to assemble. Jack

stood to his left, looking much more understated in jeans and a light blue fleece with the burgundy collar of a shirt underneath, and Hollister to his right.

Jack noticed them and waved. A few contestants turned their heads to see who the man standing by Griswold was communicating with. The nudging and pointing made Emily uncomfortable, and she dropped her waving hand. It might have been her imagination, but she thought she heard whispers of "Surly Wombat" and "Emily and James." The furtive and suspicious looks thrown her way reminded Emily that someone in this crowd had left that note in her locker. All the attention and her uncertainty about it brought Emily back to how she had felt walking through the hallways of a new school, unsure of what was in store for her.

Mr. Griswold's amplified voice boomed "Congratulations on almost making it to Unlock the Rock." There were murmurs repeating "almost," and Mr. Griswold grinned mischievously. "I say *almost* because you have one challenge left before you can claim a spot on the ferry."

Grumbles spread through the audience.

"That's right," Mr. Griswold continued. "Not all of you will be joining us on Alcatraz."

"What?!" James cried.

"Well, shoot," Nisha said softly.

"I figured we got here too easily." Maddie frowned at Mr. Griswold.

It hadn't been that easy for Emily. She mentally flicked away the seed of anxiety once again taking root.

"We've got this," Matthew said. "Let's listen."

"As you may have heard from my announcement on the Book Scavenger site, a great mystery writer has offered his involvement in our game today—"

"Errol Roy!" someone in the crowd shouted. Next to Emily, James bounced on his feet and craned his neck as if he was trying to spot the author in the crowd, even though nobody knew what he looked like.

Griswold smiled. "Now, Errol Roy is not involved in *this* task. . . ."

"Did you hear how he stressed *this*?" James whispered. "That means he *is* going to be involved later. Oh man, we've got to make it on that ferry."

". . . but Errol Roy has long credited Dashiell Hammett, the San Francisco writer famous for classic mysteries like *The Maltese Falcon*, as his inspiration and writing mentor. So in the spirit of Hammett, who was a Pinkerton detective before he became a writer, we have designed a challenge for you to earn your badge, which will be your ticket onto the ferry. If your adventure ends here, you will receive a five-dollar gift card to Hollister's new and improved bookstore, which you can bring to the grand reopening, where, perhaps, there will be signed editions of Errol Roy's novels available to you. . . ."

Mr. Griswold winked, and murmurs of interest rippled through the audience.

"What a tease," James muttered.

Mr. Griswold gestured to the row of cubicles piled with giant blocks. "What you see here are twenty sets of the same puzzle. When the horn sounds, group into teams, however you see fit—although once your team begins working on the puzzle, you may not switch. Arrange your nine blocks in three rows of three to form a picture. There are six possible images, but the correct one has to do with Dashiell Hammett. When your pieces are put together correctly, come to this platform and you will receive a card with a trivia question. Your team must answer using only your brains—no gadgets. When you think you have the answer, you get one chance to type it into that."

Next to Mr. Griswold, Hollister held up an object that looked like a label maker with a dome-shaped light-bulb attached to it.

"A green light signals the correct answer and means you have earned your detective badge and may board the ferry. A red light means your answer is incorrect and you won't be continuing in the game. However, we hope to see you at Hollister's grand-reopening party this weekend."

Jack held a horn canister above his head.

"Your time starts . . ." Mr. Griswold scanned the crowd slowly, a twinkle in his eye. "Now!"

At the bleating honk, everyone scrambled toward the sets of puzzles. James, being a fast sprinter, made it to the front of the crowd and kept going until he reached the very last pile of blocks. Emily wondered why he didn't stop at one of the closer cubicles until she passed group after group arguing with one another over who was working with whom.

"Is that Surly Wombat?" she heard as she ran past. Another voice called after her, "Want to join us, Emily?"

She kept running and didn't answer.

A middle-aged woman who wore a matching windbreaker with her male partner stood in a cubicle filled mostly with teenagers. "I can't work with children!" she cried, throwing up her hands. She called back to Mr. Griswold, "Shouldn't the adults work together?"

"However you see fit!" Mr. Griswold called back cheerfully.

"We'd be happy to switch," a familiar voice said from the next cubicle Emily passed. It was Mr. Quisling, who gave Emily a thumbs-up as she went by. His girlfriend, Miss Linden, called after her, "Good luck, Emily!"

Once Emily and the rest of her friends had reached James, he'd already moved four of the large cubes from the pile so they could spread out all the pieces for a better look. It looked like their team would only be the five of them until a woman entered their cubicle and paced around the pile of cubes, studying them. She seemed familiar, but Emily didn't know why. There wasn't anything distinguishing about her—just a lady dressed for hiking in cold weather—but Emily was still hit with an overall wave of recognition. It was one of the side effects of having moved so frequently. You saw a lot of different

faces in a lot of different places, and people started to seem familiar without you being able to remember why.

"Look at these two." Nisha pushed over one of the giant blocks until a black-and-white graphic was face-up; then she ran to another cube to do the same. "Don't these look like they'd make part of an eye?"

Matthew hoisted one of the cubes Nisha pointed to and set it next to the other. She was right; it did look like an eye. Emily clapped her hands. "Good job!"

"How do we know that's the picture we need to put together?" Maddie asked.

It was a good point. Mr. Griswold hadn't said what the final image should be. Focusing on the black-and-white pieces could be the wrong way to go; not to mention, three sides of each cube were in black and white, so figuring out which sides fit with which wasn't going to be easy.

"It doesn't matter," the strange woman said. "When you get a lead, follow it. If you stop to worry about all the possible outcomes, you'll never get anywhere."

"Who are you?" Maddie asked.

"I'm playing the game, just like you." The woman smiled coolly, unfazed by Maddie's scowling face.

"She can work with us if she wants to," James said. "Let's focus on the puzzle."

"Here's another black-and-white piece that looks like it's part of an eye," Matthew called over.

Their group went to work tipping the blocks to study the different sides, picking them up and setting them down, twisting them in different directions.

"Done!" someone called down the line of cubicles.

Emily's whole group froze. They had enough pieces pushed together to depict most of an eye and the letters *ver sleep* underneath. Because of the privacy screens, they couldn't see which group had finished or what their final puzzle looked like, but they must have gotten it right. Jack walked to the cubicle and gave a thumbs-up, and then a bunch of teenagers and Mr. Quisling and Miss Linden ran to the platform to accept the trivia card.

Even though they could have continued with their own puzzle, Emily and her friends couldn't tear their eyes from the stage. Soon one of the teenage boys ran up to Hollister and typed into the label-maker-looking gadget.

It lit up green, and Mr. Quisling and Miss Linden's group erupted into a bobbing and jumping mass.

"We have our first advancing team!" Mr. Griswold announced over the cheers. "You may proceed to the ferry!"

James raised his hands like he was trying to preemptively calm their group. "This isn't a race to be first. Let's concentrate on our own puzzle."

While Emily's team continued to work, two more teams advanced to the ferry, and three got red lights for incorrect answers and were handed gift cards as parting prizes. Raised voices carried over from two cubicles down. Although Emily couldn't see their work, it was clear from what she heard that members of that group had put half the cubes together to form part of one picture, and half the cubes together to form part of a different picture, and were now arguing over which picture they should complete.

"See?" the lady working with them said. "Distracted by possible outcomes and going nowhere."

Finally, Emily's team had a complete picture:

89

"Done!" Maddie called.

Jack ran to their station to check their work. Emily held her breath, waiting to see if the puzzle they had put together was the correct one. Jack raised a thumb in the air, and Emily exhaled. Mr. Griswold waved them over and they ran—well, all of them except the woman, but she caught up shortly after Nisha accepted an envelope from Mr. Griswold.

Nisha removed a card and read:

This symbol and slogan were the logo for the Pinkerton National Detective Agency, the first of its kind, founded in 1850. Its logo of an unblinking eye and the slogan "we never sleep" gave rise to a common nickname for detectives. This term is the solution you need to move on to the next stage of the game.

"Gumshoe?" James suggested.

"Sleuth," Nisha added.

Emily tried to think what *gumshoe* or *sleuth* had to do with seeing or sleeping. Suddenly the answer occurred to her. "It's private eye!" she hissed, excited but wanting to keep her voice low, too.

"Bingo!" the adult woman in their group said.

James ran to Hollister and punched in their answer. The light turned green, and Emily and her friends jumped up and down, cheering for themselves.

"Your badges," Mr. Griswold said, handing out silver

pins shaped like shields. The front had the words BOOK SCAVENGER DETECTIVE AGENCY on it.

James pinned his badge to his sweatshirt. "Can you believe it? We're on our way!"

Matthew spoke up for both himself and Emily. "Our first time to Alcatraz."

"Same here," Nisha said nervously.

As their group walked to the ferry, Emily said to the lady who'd worked with them, "You knew the answer. Would you have stopped us if we were going to guess wrong?"

The woman smiled wryly and said, "Still dwelling on possible outcomes, are you, Emily?"

It startled Emily to hear the woman use her name, especially given how familiar she seemed. "Do we know each other?"

The woman raised her eyebrows and said, "You were in the paper."

Of course. Emily looked down, her cheeks warming.

"I have to ask," the woman said. "How did it feel when you looked at the unbreakable code? To handle something that had once been in Twain's hands?"

"Um . . ." Emily thought back, trying to remember that day. Honestly, she wasn't sure if that thought had really occurred to her, but she could tell that wasn't the answer this grown-up wanted to hear. "It was pretty cool," she finally said. Then she added, "It's been stored at the main library for a really long time. That's where

James and I looked at it. You could go see it, too, if you wanted."

"Oh, I already have."

An unbreakable-code groupie, Emily thought. The mostly forgotten historic cipher had received a renewed burst of attention thanks to Emily and James, and Miss Linden had told them there'd been a surge in requests to see the code at the main library after it had been talked about in the news.

The woman gestured toward the ferry. "I'm going to go find a seat."

As Emily watched her walk away, she realized that while it made sense that the woman recognized Emily from the unbreakable-code coverage, that didn't explain why *Emily* felt like she knew *her* as well.

CHAPTER 13

THE GROUP of friends talked nonstop as they bounced down the awning-covered ramp to board the ferry, but Emily was distracted. It wasn't just the oddly familiar woman—it was all the looks and whispers, the strangers who seemed to know who she was.

A man wearing an orange life vest stood at the entrance to the ferry and checked for their silver badge pins before letting them on board. They crossed through the bottom level of the ferry in an unsteady zigzag pattern, thanks to the gentle bobbing of the docked boat. Two long rows of silver chairs rested back-to-back in the open middle, like someone was planning a game of musical chairs. There were only a few people down here, all Unlock the Rock players gabbing excitedly to one another.

Prerecorded safety announcements followed them outside and up the staircase that led to the second-level deck. Most people sat in the outside area, sheltered by solar panels, but Emily noticed a young girl tugging her grandfather into the small, enclosed room on the far side of the level. As their group passed by on the way to another narrower, steeper staircase, Emily heard the grandfather say, "Slow down, Iris. I'm not as spry as you."

"Let's hide our book by that window, Papa!"

The girl, Iris, held a book sealed in a plastic bag with a Book Scavenger tracking number label fixed to the front. Emily smiled when she recognized her as the same person she'd seen hunting for a golden ticket at the Grace Cathedral. It hadn't even occurred to Emily to bring a book to hide on this trip! What kind of Dupin-level book scavenger was she? Regardless, seeing Iris eager to hide a book on the ferry made Emily doubly glad she'd left the golden ticket for the girl to claim.

Emily and her friends climbed the stairs to the top level of the ferry, where most of the contestants were gathering. In the farthest corner sat that woman from their group, with her head bent over a book.

Once everyone was on board, the ship began to move backward past the warehouse docks. The water spread out like a slate-blue tablecloth with Alcatraz as a centerpiece. From this distance, the prison appeared to grow out of the rocky island base. Clouds gathered close, like they, too, were curious about what would be happening during Unlock the Rock.

Nisha stood a few feet from the railing, neck out-stretched, hugging her notebook to her chest. "Is it true there are sharks in the bay?" she asked.

"I don't think so," Emily said at the same time that her brother said, "Yes."

Nisha took another step back from the railing, like a shark was going to jump out of the water and attack them.

"Ignore my brother," Emily said. "He's teasing."

"No, it's true," Matthew said mildly, adjusting the one earbud he kept in his ear.

The ferry carved a path through choppy water. Emily found it dizzying to look down from their height to the water splashing up on the sides of the boat, so she sat on one of the hard white benches.

"What did everyone bring?" Maddie asked.

James had brought a GPS, a black light, his favorite book about codes and ciphers, a map of Alcatraz Island, and variously sized cylindrical objects.

"In case there's a scytale," he explained. It was his favorite way to encrypt a message. You wrapped a long strip of paper around something like a pencil, then wrote your message across, horizontally, with a different letter on each section of paper. When the strip of paper was unwound, the message would be garbled and could only be decoded by wrapping the paper once again around a cylinder of the same size as what was used to encode the message.

Emily shook her head. "You and your scytales."

James nudged Nisha's foot with his sneaker. "What about you?"

She held up her sketchbook, which was open to a page showing the partial profile of a nearby contestant, an older teenager who looked like she could be a model with her large brown eyes, light tan skin, and curly black hair.

"I never go anywhere without this," Nisha said.

Emily related to that. Her own Book Scavenger notebook was snug inside her backpack, as usual.

"What else?" James asked.

Nisha unzipped her backpack and tugged out a handful of knit items. "Hat, mittens, scarf, and sunscreen—"

"Sunscreen? It's overcast and practically dinnertime!" Maddie said.

Nisha shrugged. "My mom makes me bring some no matter where I'm going. She is terrified someone in our family will get cancer." She kept digging. "There's also a first aid kit and my markers and colored pencils—"

"I smell . . . spaghetti sauce or something. Did you bring food?" James reached into Nisha's backpack and pulled out a small white object that Emily first thought was a misshapen ball.

"Garlic?" James asked.

Nisha adjusted her glasses and said, very matter-of-factly, "To ward off ghosts. Just in case."

"That only works on vampires," Matthew said.

Nisha plucked the garlic from James's fingers and dropped it back in her bag. "I also have lemon juice—in case we need to write something in invisible ink—and a battery-operated heat gun in case we need to reveal it. And spare batteries and my mom's digital kitchen scale."

"That is one random assortment of stuff," Matthew commented.

"Well, then, what about you, mysterious older brother?" Maddie asked. "What's in your backpack?"

Matthew had brought a calculator, a flashlight, and a small camera in case he had to turn in his cell phone. There was a large bag of Goldfish crackers, which made Emily roll her eyes because it took up so much space. "And a Swiss Army knife and a lock-picking kit. You know, in case we need to unlock something."

Emily and her friends were quiet a minute, staring at Matthew's open backpack.

"A lock-picking kit for Unlock the Rock. Why didn't we think of that?" Nisha said what they all were thinking.

"What about you, Maddie?" Emily asked.

Emily hadn't realized how bulging Maddie's backpack was until she watched her slide it from her back to the floor with a loud thump.

"Here's what I brought: a compass, another calculator, another Alcatraz map from the tour I took years ago, *Alcatraz: Believe It or Not* by T. C. Baker, *Eyewitness on Alcatraz* by Jolene Babyak . . ."

She continued to list several more books as well as colored pens, highlighters, an eraser, Post-its, and a mini stapler.

"E-books would have made your backpack way lighter," James observed.

"Maybe, but I have an excellent memory for things I've read in a physical book. If you had a digital copy and I had a physical copy of the same book and someone timed us to see who could find answers to questions the fastest, I would beat you, no question about it."

James raised his eyebrows. "We might need to test that theory, Maddie."

"What about you?" Matthew asked Emily. "You haven't shared."

Emily opened her bag to show that, in addition to her Book Scavenger notebook, she'd brought her new night-vision goggles and even more books than Maddie had, among other things. But before she got to any of that, a piece of paper fluttered out. She recognized the print on it before she'd even picked it up off the floor. It was another note made of cutout letters, like the ones she and James had found in their lockers earlier that week. This one read:

YOU SHOULDN'T BE HERE

CHAPTER 14

"ANOTHER ONE?" James said.

"Another what?" Maddie strained to see.

"You didn't get another one?" Emily asked.

"Not this time," he said.

"What's going on?" Maddie asked, visibly annoyed at the cryptic way they were talking.

"Someone stuck this in my backpack," Emily explained.

"We both got one like this before," James added.

Maddie, Nisha, and Matthew crowded closer to look at the paper.

"Someone's been threatening you?" Matthew asked.

"Trying to scare us away from the competition today," James said.

Emily didn't know if it was the new creepy note appearing in her backpack, but she couldn't shake the feeling that someone was watching her. She scanned the crowded ferry deck until she spotted the same girl Nisha had been sketching, who was now watching their group. As soon as Emily made eye contact, the girl exclaimed loudly enough to turn heads, "Oh. My. Gosh."

The girl repeated this and dramatically walked toward them, slowly, with her hands up as if she were examining her manicure. People quieted as she cut a path through the crowd. The metal charms on her bracelet tinkled with every step.

"Hey, she goes to my school," Matthew said.

"You are *not* Emily Crane and James Lee," she said, turning even more heads. "Tell me you two are not the amazing duo who solved Mr. Griswold's *Gold-Bug* mystery. And cracked the unbreakable code. It cannot be you. Can. Not."

"Uh . . ." Emily and James looked at each other, not sure what to say. It was clear the girl knew who they were.

"I have to shake your hand." The girl's long nails dug into Emily's wrist when she clutched her palm. "My name is Fiona Duncan."

Matthew stood up. "You go to Carver High, right? I'm Emily's *older* brother," he said. "I helped them with the—"

Fiona ignored Matthew and threw an arm around James's shoulders, squeezing him tightly to her side. "You are as adorable in person as you were on the news!

Look at how your hair pops up!" Fiona pressed down Steve, then let go. The tuft of hair popped back up like an inflatable bop bag.

James grimaced and mouthed, *Help me*, to Emily, who giggled in response.

Keeping her arm around James's shoulder, Fiona said, "So, gang, what's the plan? Do you know what we're in for this afternoon?"

James ducked free from her arm and said, "We know as much as you."

Fiona cocked an eyebrow. "Sure you do. Stick with that story if you want." She grinned. "I would if I was in your shoes."

"Fiona!"

A slightly older version of Fiona marched over.

"Yes, Mom?" Fiona cooed.

"Your mom?!" Maddie said. "She doesn't look that old."

Fiona's mother's eyes settled on Maddie, a sly smile on her face. "Aren't you sweet. Thank you, dear. Yes, I'm Mrs. Duncan, Fiona's mother," she said. "I'm sorry to interrupt, but I need to discuss something with my daughter." She looped her hand under Fiona's biceps and tightened her grip to pull her away. "Now," she said through gritted teeth.

As they walked away, Emily could hear Mrs. Duncan hiss, "I leave you for one minute and you can't follow a simple direction? I told you not to talk to anyone."

Their voices faded into the chatter around them.

"Well, that was weird," James said, and then Fiona shrieked loudly enough to make everyone on the deck go silent. For a wild second, Emily worried that Fiona's mom had hurt her daughter, but the two stood feet apart.

"What is it now?!" Fiona's mother cried, her voice half perplexed, half exasperated.

"My bracelet!" Fiona wailed, holding up one hand to show a bare wrist. "It's gone!" Emily remembered the tinkling charms when Fiona had approached them only minutes ago. The news spread like a ripple across the deck that somebody had lost a piece of jewelry. People surrounded Fiona asking what they could do.

"We should help her find it," Emily said to her friends, scanning the floor around them. "I saw it on her wrist when she walked over here. It must be nearby."

"Why help *her*? That girl was obnoxious." Maddie jutted her chin toward the commotion. "There are plenty of wannabe detectives already on the case."

"Well, I'm helping look," Emily said. Matthew, James, and Nisha joined in the search. Maddie sighed and stared half-heartedly at the floor, scuffing her foot at a random leaf. Practically the whole top deck full of people searched for the lost bracelet. Even the lady who'd worked with Emily and her friends on the first challenge had put down her book and was prowling around with everyone else.

While people scanned the deck around her, Fiona collapsed onto a bench and wailed, "It's gone!"

"Are you sure you wore it today?" asked a woman kindly.

"Of course she's sure," Fiona's mother snapped. "She wears it every day."

The woman's helpful expression disappeared, like a candle snuffed out, and the contestants drifted away from Fiona and her mother to resume their own conversations.

"That girl thinks she's the star of her own show. You can just tell," Maddie said.

"I thought she was trying to be nice," Matthew replied.

Maddie snorted. "You would think that."

"Her mom was something else," James said. "I feel sorry for Fiona."

"I bet her mom is *overworked and underappreciated*." Maddie's tone was mocking, like she was parroting something she'd heard an adult say many times over. Then she shook her head like she was tossing away thoughts of Fiona and straightened her shoulders. "We're going to be at Alcatraz soon. We need to focus. Get our heads in the game. Quick! What year did the federal penitentiary close?"

They stared at Maddie with blank expressions.

"Didn't you guys study about the island at all? It was 1963," she answered. "Name one of the most notorious inmates."

Simultaneously James, Nisha, and Emily shouted, "Al Capone!"

"Did you guys read that book, too?" Nisha asked.

"Yes, and one better," Emily replied. She unzipped the small pocket on her backpack and pulled out her tattered copy of *Al Capone Does My Shirts*. "I brought it."

James grinned. "You and your books."

"You bring your scytales," Emily said, "and I'll bring my books."

CHAPTER 15

AS THE FERRY approached Alcatraz, everyone clustered along the railings to get a view of the island. The clouds Emily had seen from a distance had settled into a thick fog, creeping around the old, decrepit buildings that dotted the island.

Once the ferry docked, everyone funneled down the staircases to the main level. Emily and her friends were shuffling toward the exit when a kid stepped directly into her path and jabbed Emily's side with his elbow as he moved ahead.

"Hey!" Emily said.

"Sorry." The boy's tone didn't sound at all remorseful. He sneered at her and said to his two friends, both a head taller than him, "Oh, look, it's Swamp Bat."

There was only one person on the Book Scavenger website who called her that: Bookacuda.

She remembered that his profile said he was an eighth grader, but he didn't look it. Bookacuda was about her size, with sandy-brown hair and pale skin that made his freckles look like flecks of paint.

Emily rolled her eyes and focused on moving with the herd of people. She didn't want to give him the satisfaction of letting him think she cared.

"Who are you?" James asked, irritation in his voice.

"This is Bookacuda," the girl in the trio answered.

"Are we supposed to be impressed?" Maddie asked.

"If you're not now, you will be," Bookacuda said. He turned back to Emily. "We'll see how far luck gets you today, Swamp Bat."

Emily knew the best thing to do with trolls was ignore them, so she did, but his dig still got under her skin. They also brought to mind the note left in her backpack—YOU SHOULDN'T BE HERE. Earlier that week, when Emily couldn't figure out that entry puzzle, she'd felt like it was her big secret. She'd felt like a fraud.

Now she wondered, had that been obvious to everyone all along?

Bookacuda and his friends pushed ahead and disappeared into the stream of people exiting the ferry. The Unlock the Rock contestants gathered in the shadow of an old building, four stories tall with windows that stared blankly out to the restless water. A black-and-white penitentiary sign hung on the concrete façade with the words *Indians Welcome* scrawled above in dark red paint. To Emily, it looked anything but welcoming.

Shielding her eyes from the sun, she took in the intimidatingly tall silhouette of a guardhouse on stilts. Seagulls swooped around it like vultures. The structure was empty, but Emily could imagine being back in time when a guard was stationed up there with a gun watching over the island.

"This is creepy," Nisha whispered, turning in a half circle.

"Alcatraz is one of the top tourist destinations in the United States," Maddie said. After a beat she added, "But yeah, this is kind of creepy."

A woman wearing a park-ranger hat and bulky green jacket stepped forward from her post next to a kiosk that held maps and brochures. "It's history, that's what it is," she said, and waved Emily's group and the rest of the contestants over to the line of trams that would drive them up the incline to the prison at the top.

"Let's find a seat in the front," Maddie said.

The front tramcar had four benches: one facing forward, one facing backward, and in between those, like the long part of a capital letter *I*, two more benches placed back-to-back. The whole train was pulled by a tiny truck only big enough to hold the driver. Emily and her friends were stacking their backpacks on the rear bench of the head passenger car when Bookacuda and his boy and girl bookends took the open seats.

"Hey, dude, we were going to sit there," Matthew said.

"Was this reserved for you?" Bookacuda asked. He crossed his arms and looked up at Matthew.

"Don't be a jerk," Emily said.

"I'm not the one acting like a Book Scavenger princess. Are you going to expect special treatment the entire game?"

"I wasn't . . ." Heat raced up Emily's neck to her cheeks. "I don't want special treatment."

One of Bookacuda's friends—the boy with the curly pile of hair on top of his head—poked him in the ribs and then nodded to something behind Emily.

Bookacuda jumped up from his seat and broke into a wide grin. "Mr. Griswold!" He waved enthusiastically and extended his hand as the publisher approached. "It's a pleasure to meet you. I'm Bookacuda, the youngest Book Scavenger at Sherlock level."

Mr. Griswold clutched his hand and smiled. "Wonderful, wonderful. So glad you are joining us," he said. Noticing Emily, James, and Matthew, his smile grew even wider. "My advisory team! Hello, you three."

Standing behind Mr. Griswold, Bookacuda scowled and turned away, his friends following him. Emily tried not to show her delight.

The elderly man who'd walked up with Mr. Griswold gave a tight-lipped smile and stepped past the young contestants to seat himself in the front car facing the water. Hollister appeared, affectionately mussing Matthew's green-sprout hair as he stepped through their group to sit with Jack on the bench behind the elderly man.

"I hope we didn't scare your friends away." Mr. Griswold gestured to Bookacuda and his sidekicks, who were now halfway down the line of trams, looking for other seats.

Emily didn't bother explaining that Bookacuda wasn't a friend.

Maddie had claimed benches for Emily and the others in the second passenger car, but they left their backpacks where they'd piled them on the bench in the back of Mr. Griswold's.

Soon the trucks towing the tramcars puttered to life, and they were bobbing and bumping up the paved trail. The main cell house had been built on the crest of the

small island, and the path to get there was a steep set of switchbacks.

The static amplification of a ranger's voice came through speakers, telling them that they were driving through the sally port, an arched opening in an old building, which dated back to the 1800s, and then past the shell of another building that had suffered a fire in the 1970s. The view down to the gray water below was a sheer hillside overrun with tangled greenery.

Nisha, who was sitting behind Emily, said, "I heard there's a dungeon in the prison."

"A dungeon?" Emily repeated, turning to her friend. The word gave her visions of skeletons chained to stone walls. Nisha nodded emphatically, then shivered.

"Why do you believe this stuff?" Maddie said. "You're so gullible, Nisha."

"She's right, though," James said. "There is a dungeon."

"There is?!" Emily and Maddie said in unison. Matthew popped his earbud out to listen better. The tram was making another turn when James said, "It's not like it was a torture chamber or anything. At least, I don't think—"

Emily lurched in her seat as the truck driving their tram jerked to the right, then slammed into a rock retaining wall. People shouted and shrieked. The passenger car in front—with Mr. Griswold, his friend, Hollister, and Jack—tipped toward the wall. Hollister gripped the pole next to him and jumped to the ground as his bench began to rise. Jack followed suit. The back-packs Emily and her friends had left piled on the rear bench tumbled to the ground, followed by Mr. Griswold and his friend, who slid from their bench like grapes rolling off a spoon.

"Mr. Griswold!" Emily shouted.

The two men landed in a crouch and threw their arms over their heads, bracing for the impact of their tramcar as it continued to fall forward, threatening to pin them against the retaining wall.

CHAPTER 16

WHEN ERROL ROY was thrown from the tramcar to the ground, his arms instinctively went up, protecting his head. There were shouts and shrieks. Luggage from his tram fell in a series of thuds. Metal creaked. He closed his eyes to brace for impact, cursing this gloomy island, but the blow Errol anticipated didn't come.

He opened his eyes and realized that his tramcar had remained suspended above his head. Hollister and Jack had managed to jump out and grab hold of the poles to keep it from capsizing completely. Others ran forward to help right it. The train of passenger cars behind his had stayed upright in the crash, although people were jumping out, buzzing with confusion and concern.

Errol had begun to straighten when he spotted a scrap of paper by his foot. Cutout letters spelled the words:

Errol's breath caught in his throat.

He picked up the note. It was crumpled and smeared with dirt, slightly damp from the fog, but otherwise it felt like a fresh piece of paper. This wasn't litter that had been neglected on the trail. He folded it into his pocket.

Errol stood and faced Mr. Griswold, who was dusting himself off. The publisher's colorful top hat had been crushed in the fall, making his getup look more ridiculous than usual when he placed it back on his head.

"Are you all right?" Mr. Griswold asked, placing a shaking hand on Errol's shoulder.

Errol's body would be scolding him for days to come, but that wasn't what concerned him at the moment.

"I'm fine," he replied. But he wasn't. He wasn't fine at all. When he'd stepped from the ferry onto this cursed island, he'd felt the first drips of regret, which now trickled through his body like a poison.

Mr. Griswold went to check on the driver, who was being looked over by paramedics. It figured that Griswold or Alcatraz would have emergency services on hand.

Jack stepped over the coupling that joined the passenger cars and said to Errol in a low voice, "The driver is fine, although embarrassed. He'll have a case of whiplash, I'm sure." He pointed to one of the park rangers, who held a wooden post with nails sticking from it. "He swerved to miss driving over that."

Hollister shook his head. "Where did something like that come from, anyway?"

Jack pointed up the sheer hillside to a chain-link fence covered in a green tarp. A sign posted on the side of the tarp read: DANGER! HARD HAT AREA. "A ranger said there's a reconstruction project under way on the island, so maybe a cart was trucking debris down the hill and that post fell off the back, or it somehow rolled down the hillside."

"I'm glad nobody's hurt," Hollister said.

Errol kept quiet. He was deep in thought about the note in his pocket. Had it been meant for him? How had it been delivered in that moment? Had someone placed it on his person and then it fell out in the crash?

Soon everyone had reboarded the tram, and they continued the drive to the cell house. Neither Mr. Griswold, Jack, nor Hollister seemed to consider that what happened might be anything other than an accident. But because of the note, Errol couldn't help wondering if someone was sending him a message.

Could somebody on this island know who he was and what he was *really* here to do?

CHAPTER 17

EMILY COULDN'T STOP replaying the visual of Mr. Griswold falling and the paralyzing fear that he'd be crushed. Fortunately, nobody had been seriously hurt in the accident, but the scare had unnerved her, even after everyone was back in their seats and they had resumed their uphill trek.

Their tram bumped extra high, and Emily gripped the pole next to her before realizing there had only been a rut in the path. She tried to distract herself from this gloomy anxiousness settling over her by concentrating on her friends' conversation. James was speculating about how Errol Roy might be involved in the game.

"What if Errol Roy is a she?" Maddie asked James.

He frowned. "What do you mean?"

"You said nobody knows what he looks like, right? He's a big mystery?"

"But . . . he's a man," James insisted. "Probably a man in his sixties, since he's been publishing books for the last forty or so years. It's a known fact."

"It's an *assumed* fact," Maddie said. "She could be using a pen name."

Nisha nodded, mulling over Maddie's theory. "It would be a clever way to stay hidden in public."

James plucked at Steve distractedly as he considered this idea.

"Does it matter?" Emily asked. "It doesn't change the books."

"No, it doesn't matter. It's just . . . I mean, I always pictured him a certain way. Like a secret agent, wearing a dark suit and sunglasses."

"He might still look like that," Nisha said encouragingly. "But a girl version."

"None of you have even read his books," James muttered. "It's like I'm imagining dragons and you're all telling me how mine should look, but you don't even care about the dragons in the first place."

Matthew placed a hand on James's shoulder. "We'll let you have your dragons, man," he said in mock seriousness.

Listening to her friends' banter helped ease Emily's gloomy feeling. The tram came to a stop outside the prison, and the contestants stepped off. Emily hugged her arms to herself and ducked her head to brace against the chilly wind that had kicked up. An American flag raised in front of the cell house flapped back and forth. Far across the water, through breaks in the fog, she could see the San Francisco skyline, which looked miniature from so far away. It occurred to her that without the ferry they would be totally stranded. There was no bus or cab or BART or walking route she could take home at her convenience.

Maddie picked up her backpack from their pile, then gave it a second look.

"Wait, this is yours, Emily." She lifted the other backpacks from the bench and handed them out. Matthew accepted the last one and Maddie looked at the empty bench. "Where's mine?"

They made a show of looking for the backpack, even though the tramcar was clearly empty.

"My backpack is missing!" Maddie said.

"It probably fell off in the tram accident," James pointed out.

"Everything was picked up from the ground. I'm sure of it," Maddie insisted. "Somebody stole it!"

"You had something stolen, too?" Fiona walked up, her eyes wide with concern.

"Mr. Griswold!" Maddie called to the book publisher, who was walking toward the prison with the men from his tram. Emily and the rest of their group followed behind as she ran over to him. "Mr. Griswold, my backpack is missing!"

"Missing?" Mr. Griswold repeated.

"We put our backpacks on the back of your tramcar, but hers isn't there," Emily explained.

"It has to be somewhere. How would a whole backpack go missing?" James asked.

"That's what I'd like to know," Maddie said.

"Someone stole it, that's how," Fiona piped up. She'd tagged along, much to Emily's annoyance.

Maddie—who hadn't seemed to care much for Fiona the first time around on the ferry—now gave a perfunctory nod of agreement. Emily felt bad that Maddie couldn't find her backpack, but they'd been with their bags the whole time they'd been on the island. James was right; it had to be somewhere.

"Why don't I go back down and take a look while you get the game under way?" Jack offered to Mr. Griswold. "See if it fell off the tram or maybe was left at the dock."

"I know exactly where I left it," Maddie said. "It was right between Emily's and Nisha's backpacks, and it's not there. *Her* bracelet was stolen on the ferry"—she jabbed a finger at Fiona—"and now my backpack. There's a thief playing your game, Mr. Griswold."

"Well, I certainly hope not," he replied. "Don't worry, Maddie. Jack will find it."

Maddie pursed her lips, clearly skeptical, but there was nothing else to be done.

"Thank you, Jack!" James called after the publisher's assistant as he walked away, and he nudged Maddie to do the same.

She nudged him back but also called out, "Thank you!"

They walked to the main entrance of the cell house, passing another burnt shell of a building and the old lighthouse tower. The sun glowed in the fog like a flashlight shining through a sheet, casting an orange aura in the sky as it inched behind the immense prison building. Beige paint peeled off the exterior in chunks, revealing gray patches of concrete. The entry doors were propped open in a way that might have been welcoming on another day, in another setting, but not today. Instead of walking into Alcatraz feeling giddy and excited to play Mr. Griswold's game, Emily felt wary, guarded, and unsure of what might happen next.

CHAPTER 18

T HE CELL HOUSE was frigid, even chillier than
being outside, although maybe it was the cold gray
cement and cinder block that made Emily feel that way.
She tucked her fists inside the sleeves of her fleece jacket
and stared down an aisle of metal bars with jail cells
stacked three stories high to the ceiling. Even the skylights
on the ceiling had bars covering them. The cells were
stark: concrete walls painted hospital green and cream,
barely big enough to hold a cot, sink, toilet, and small
tabletop that folded down from the wall. A yellow bulb
glowed in each cell, and in any other setting it might
have struck Emily as cozy, but here it felt—

"Creeeeeeepy," Nisha whispered, as though reading
Emily's mind.

Some cells were completely empty. Others had props
inside, like a stack of folded sheets on the mattress or an
open booklet on the table. Emily was startled to realize

that a few cells even contained real live men dressed in prison garb. One lay on his cot reading a book. Another worked on a painting. A third strummed a guitar. Emily had heard the tranquil melody when they'd first entered the cell house, but she'd assumed it came from speakers. It was disconcerting to see people inside these cells, even though Emily knew they must be actors hired for Mr. Griswold's game. Footsteps overhead prompted her to look up. A man dressed as a guard strolled along the walkway that ran in front of the cells on the second level.

Emily shivered, squeezing her shoulders up. As the long stream of contestants filed past the cells, none of the actors called out or gave any sign that they'd even noticed the sixty-some people traipsing down the corridor. Mr. Griswold didn't interact with the actors, either. He simply led the crowd toward a large room with a sign over the door that read DINING HALL, the taps of his cane echoing in the cavernous space.

Matthew stopped walking just outside the entrance to the dining hall, staring at the round clock that hung above the door with a placard that read TIMES SQUARE.

"Is that really the time?" Matthew asked.

The Roman numerals showed it was 2:40.

"No, it couldn't be," Emily answered. They'd started the puzzle on the pier around four thirty. There was no way that was the correct time. "It must be broken."

From inside the dining hall there was the *dum-dum* of another microphone being tapped. They hurried inside with the rest of the contestants.

The dining hall was a large expanse of space, with tall windows lining the right and left sides of the room. The windows were dirty and covered with bars, which diffused the light coming through. All the way in the back was a kitchen, also behind bars, from which warm smells drifted forward to greet them. A menu board hung above the kitchen, but Emily was too far away to read it.

Mr. Griswold stood on a raised platform and waited for people to assemble. His colorful outfit seemed wildly out of place here, like doing the hokey-pokey in a grave-yard. More "prisoners" were seated at some of the round tables set up around the room. Other tables were empty or had items set out on top.

Just like those in the cell house, these prisoners didn't appear to notice anything outside of the game of dominoes they played or the meal they poked at. Men and women wearing bright yellow vests that read SECURITY stood around the edges of the room. Emily wasn't sure if they were also actors in the game or real security, but either way, their presence made her feel even more anxious, like they were a reminder that things could go wrong.

Mr. Griswold leaned both hands on his cane and spoke into a microphone. "Shall we get started?"

Murmurs of enthusiasm rippled through the crowd, and in his booming, theatrical voice Mr. Griswold said, "Welcome to Unlock the Rock!"

Emily joined her friends in clapping, but looked around the crowd with a bit of wonder that being in a former prison didn't seem to be getting to other contestants the way it was for her. She reminded herself: *This is just a game.*

Mr. Griswold spoke again. "Thank you all for joining us for what I'm certain will be a memorable, challenging, and fun evening. We have exciting surprises for you—"

"Errol Roy!" someone shouted, maybe the same person as earlier at the pier.

Mr. Griswold smiled, his bristly mustache lifting like a happy broom, but he continued as if he hadn't heard.

"Regardless of how you fare today, everyone is invited to the grand reopening of Hollister's bookstore next Sunday. Bring your entry ticket and Book Scavenger badge from today and you will receive a ten-dollar gift certificate for purchase of anything in the store. And, of course, the winner—or winners—today will receive a year's subscription to Hollister's Book of the Month club, as well as having the honor of naming a shelf in the store that will be stocked with their book recommendations."

One lady shouted, "Hollister!" which was followed by people whistling, applauding, and cheering. The bookseller tipped a finger from his temple to the air in a thank-you salute.

"You may have noticed there are others with us here on Alcatraz." Mr. Griswold gestured toward the actors scattered around the room. An inmate seated at a table nearby mugged a glowering expression for the crowd, and

Mr. Griswold hurried to add, "I assure you these people are here to help you in your quest, whether or not they seem, uh . . ." He looked nervously at the still-scowling prisoner. People in the audience laughed. "Whether or not they seem helpful," Mr. Griswold continued.

"The park rangers, guards, and prisoners have important information to share with you. Seek them out and you might make quicker progress through the game. But be forewarned. . . ."

Mr. Griswold held up a finger and scanned the room, making sure everyone was listening. "There are often tricks involved in accessing the information these helpers have to give, and it's up to you to figure out what those tricks are. It's also worth noting that not all of the clues you uncover tonight—whether through speaking with the helpful prisoners and guards and rangers, or through puzzles you uncover on your own—will lead you toward the solution of tonight's game.

"Also, very important, if a room has a 'Do Not Enter' sign posted, that is not a prop for the game. Heed the sign and *do not enter*! These signs are there for your safety and for preserving and respecting the historical integrity of this island. We tried to make it fairly obvious what can be handled and what should be observed, but if you have any questions, please ask. There are one or two puzzles that might lead you to an outside location, but for the most part everything for the game will be found inside this cell house building.

"And, of course, there should be no disrupting of the

puzzles. Leave everything as you found it for other play-ers to discover and solve in their own time.

"Now, I am sure you are most interested in hearing what your task will be tonight. Not only will you be solving an original Errol Roy mystery, as you already know, but the author himself is here to explain your mis-sion. It's my pleasure to welcome . . . Errol Roy!"

If a room full of people could collectively gasp, that's exactly what they did. Voices began to whisper, "He's really here?" and "I knew it!"

The man who'd sat next to Mr. Griswold on the tram stepped onto the stage. He held up an envelope in greet-ing, only a slight smile on his face. He waited for the confused and excited chatter to die down.

"That's him?"

"Errol Roy?"

"Is that an actor?"

The man held the microphone to his lips. His voice was a little shaky when he said, "Yes, it's me."

The room went crazy with cheers and jumping. Errol Roy's eyes widened at the response and he took a step backward. Emily expected James to flip out, but he simply stood with his mouth hanging open, staring at Errol Roy.

Emily nudged him. "He's here!"

"I imagined him a lot younger," he finally said.

Nisha flipped to a clean sheet in her sketchbook and started drawing a portrait of the author.

"Well, you were right that he's a dude," Matthew said.

Maddie snorted a laugh.

"Aren't you excited?" Emily asked James. "You get to meet him!"

James continued to stare at the author. "Yeah . . . I just . . . I need to do some mental reprogramming." He blinked repeatedly like his eyes were the shutter on a camera.

Taking in the shaggy-haired, bearded elderly man with loose pants and a sweatshirt with cable cars on it covering a protruding belly, Emily could see how this person might not match the slick secret agent that James had had in mind.

Errol Roy cleared his throat. "Thank you." Instead of looking at the crowd, he looked up to the water-stained ceiling. "I want to make it clear from the start that Garrison Griswold and his team did the bulk of work to arrange this for you. Any gratitude you feel for this event should be directed to them. I can only take credit for one small part: the story I've prepared to share with you. I also want to make it clear that I, and I alone, am responsible for that. I proposed this collaboration with Mr. Griswold on the one condition that nobody see a preview of this story in advance of you all."

"It's true!" Mr. Griswold chimed in. "I am in as much suspense as you! I love an Errol Roy mystery, and I'm confident we're in for a treat."

Fiona's mother called out from where she stood in the front row, "You all deserve a round of applause!" She raised her hands above her head to model clapping, and everyone politely joined in. Mr. Griswold extended his hands first to Errol Roy and then to Hollister, standing off to the side, to indicate his appreciation for them.

Errol Roy pulled a handkerchief from his pocket and dabbed it against his forehead. When the noise died down he said, "I'd like to begin my story."

James's shock had worn off, and he advised their group, "Pay attention. I've read all his books, and if there's one thing I know, it's that the clues are often hidden in plain sight. You don't want to miss anything."

Everyone stilled to listen, even the people standing all the way back in the kitchen, waiting to serve food. On the other side of the room, Emily spotted Mr. Quisling and Miss Linden on the edges of the crowd. The librarian leaned her back against the teacher, her head tucking under his chin. The faint melody of the strumming guitar drifted in, and a plane rumbled by outside, but otherwise the prison was filled with an anticipatory quiet.

"The format a story is told in makes a difference— anyone who has both read a book and seen its movie adaptation knows this. Your experience of a story is not the same reading it versus watching it unfold cinematically." When Errol Roy spoke, he rocked ever so slightly and didn't seem to know where to look. He addressed first the lights hanging from the ceiling, then the chipped concrete floor. "The opportunity to tell you a story using the unusual format today's event offers, with an interactive reader experience, was one I couldn't resist."

He looked at the audience now, but his gaze jumped from face to face, almost as if he were searching for someone among the crowd. He looked down to his feet and stayed like that, not moving and not talking, for a beat, then another, then another. He was silent so long, people shifted and exchanged looks with one another. Finally Errol Roy spoke again.

"I'm not comfortable with this. . . ." He emphasized *this* by moving his hands in circles like he was clearing two spots on a foggy window. "This . . . public speaking. I apologize, but I need to read the rest of what I've prepared."

He opened the envelope he held and with a shaking hand removed a typed piece of paper. Watching Errol Roy reminded Emily of being in the third grade, when she'd had to present her oral report on Laura Ingalls Wilder to the class in costume, one week after she'd moved to South Dakota. She felt sympathy for Roy.

"A mystery has been laid out for you tonight, told in the form of puzzles," Errol Roy read. "Four puzzles make up the solution you seek. Some puzzles are red herrings. Use your wits to determine which puzzles deserve your attention and which can be ignored. You are free to work alone, in pairs, teams, however you'd like. As an extra incentive, if someone is able to uncover the solution by eight p.m., I will donate one hundred thousand dollars to Hollister's bookstore."

Gasps erupted from the crowd, including from Emily and James, who exchanged incredulous looks with each other. Hollister himself must not have known this until just now. He staggered backward playfully, then jogged to Errol Roy and swung an arm around his shoulders. The bookseller leaned to the mic and said, "What are we standing around here for? Let's find those puzz—"

Sirens cut him off mid-sentence. Emily's hands flew up to her ears. Why were so many things going wrong today? Lights flashed, and the sound of metal locks clamping shut thundered across the room. People shrieked and shouted out questions.

"What's going on?"

"Is this part of the game?"

"Mr. Griswold, explain yourself!"

CHAPTER 19

OVER A LOUDSPEAKER a monotone woman's voice intoned, "A prisoner has escaped Alcatraz. Lockdown has been initiated. Repeat: A prisoner has escaped his cell. Lockdown has been initiated."

The panic subdued to nervous laughter and the crowd refocused on the author. Errol Roy mopped his brow again with his handkerchief. He really didn't look well, Emily thought, like maybe somebody should bring him a chair to sit in.

"This is where your mystery begins," Roy said. "Identify the escaped prisoner by solving the correct puzzles. After I read your first clue, the game will start."

Roy folded up the letter-sized paper he had read from and tried to slide it back into the envelope, but because of his shaking hands it took him several attempts. Emily felt like she was watching the slow unwrapping of a gift as she waited to hear the first clue.

Finally, Errol Roy reached into his pocket and withdrew an index card.

He read aloud: "'I know your secret.'"

Hums of speculation spread throughout the audience as the couples and groups considered what that first clue could mean.

"Are we supposed to start?" Nisha asked.

"How is that a clue?" Maddie said.

"Maybe we should talk to one of the prisoners or guards," James suggested. "Mr. Griswold said the actors are here to help."

Emily hadn't stopped watching Errol Roy, who was still looking at the first clue card. He dropped it to the floor like he'd been burned and turned to Mr. Griswold. "Is this some kind of joke?"

Mr. Griswold's smile disappeared. "No, I . . ." He looked questioningly to Hollister, who gave a slight shake of his head.

Errol Roy's finger wavered over the discarded note. His voice was raised, and several contestants looked up from their discussions, uncertain if this was something they should listen to.

"That isn't what it's supposed to say," Errol Roy said. "Did you switch my card?"

The audience stilled, everyone's attention now fully back on the author. His face bloomed magenta. "I can't be here right now. I need to go somewhere else."

"Mr. Roy, please." Mr. Griswold looked again to Hollister, who shrugged helplessly.

Roy walked to the edge of the platform and stepped down, right in front of Fiona, whose mother held up a phone, trying to take a selfie with him in the background.

"I told you he'd be here, Fiona," Mrs. Duncan announced in her very loud voice.

Errol Roy stopped walking and turned slowly to face her. His movements vacuumed the room into silence. "How would you know that?" His low voice carried across the expansive cement box of a room.

Mrs. Duncan sputtered, "Well, I mean . . . it was announced!"

Errol Roy stepped closer. "Did you leave that note?"

"I . . ." Flummoxed, the woman lifted her phone. "I was only taking a picture. I'm a fan."

Errol Roy glanced briefly at her screen and winced. "Delete that," he said, and stalked out of the dining hall.

"Mr. Roy!" Mr. Griswold hurried after him, calling over his shoulder, "Hollister, can you take over for me?"

Jack entered the room, a backpack in hand, and looked on, bewildered, as Errol Roy marched past, followed by Mr. Griswold.

"He found it!" Maddie crowed, and went to retrieve her backpack.

"What do we do now?" Nisha asked. "That couldn't have been part of the game, right?"

"I don't think so," James said uncertainly. He frowned at the wake of his literary hero.

The contestants were buzzing with confusion over

what to do. What an odd start to the event, Emily thought. The tram accident and now this mix-up with Errol Roy's clue, and the author himself didn't seem to want to be here.

Hollister stood alone on the stage. He scooped up the notecard Mr. Roy had dropped and slipped it into his own pocket, then stepped to the microphone. "Well," he said. "That was unexpected."

Nervous titters spread throughout the crowd.

A woman raised her hand but spoke before Hollister could call on her. "Does this mean the game is canceled?"

"Yeah," someone else said. "Do we still get the gift cards?"

Hollister tugged at the collar of his shirt. "Of course the offer still stands for the gift cards. Simply bring your entry ticket to my store Sunday. As for the game, I'm, uh, not sure how . . . uh, let's give Mr. Griswold a minute here."

Maddie returned wearing her backpack.

"Where was it?" Nisha asked, sliding her glasses up her nose.

"It was on the dock!" Maddie threw her hands in the air. "How is that even possible? You all saw me put it on the tram." She slid one strap off and held the bag to her front as she rifled through her belongings.

"Maybe it fell off when the tram started to move," Nisha suggested.

"And none of us noticed?" Maddie said. She tugged

the zipper closed. "Whatever. I have it back and nothing's missing."

"All the more reason to think it wasn't stolen," James said.

"Well, I didn't leave it behind."

"You two like to argue, don't you?" Matthew observed.

"It's their thing," Nisha said.

In unison Maddie and James said, "It is not our thing!"

Nisha gave Matthew a *See? I told you* look.

Mr. Griswold stepped back in the dining room, caught Hollister's eye, and rolled his hand in a *keep going* gesture. Hollister spoke into the microphone but directed his question to Mr. Griswold. "The game? We still on?"

Mr. Griswold nodded and disappeared back into the hallway. Hollister's face split into a smile, although Emily thought it looked a little stretched tight.

"All right, folks! The game's still on."

"How do we get started?" someone called out.

"Yeah," someone else piped up. "Errol Roy said he was reading the first clue, but then that wasn't it."

"Oh. Well." Hollister pulled the notecard from his pocket and glanced at it quickly before putting it back. "What I know is this: There are puzzles all around the cell house. Wherever you're allowed access, it's likely you'll find one. Some of them are obvious; some of them are not. And like Mr. Roy said, not all of them will be relevant to the solution. I don't know what the first clue was *supposed* to say, but I do know there are at least three puzzles—or parts of a puzzle—in this very room right now. Hopefully that's enough to get you started."

Hollister hadn't even stopped talking before the dining hall started churning like a blender on low, everyone eager to begin. All the different voices echoed off the cinder-block walls and high ceilings.

The actors in the room playing prisoners and guards, and the Alcatraz park rangers, were swarmed with contestants wanting to ask them questions, hoping for the hints and clues Mr. Griswold had said they had to offer. A line formed at the food service in the back as well.

"What's our plan?" Nisha's sketchbook was flipped to a blank page and her marker was poised and ready. She looked to Emily, who looked to James, who looked to Matthew, who was checking the time on a clock hung next to a window.

"The plan is to look for puzzles, duh," Maddie replied. To Emily and James she asked, "Are you two absolutely positive you don't know anything about how this is supposed to work? Like if it's worth waiting in one of those lines to talk to a prisoner, or how we even find the puzzles or tell which ones are part of Mr. Roy's solution?"

"For the millionth time, *no*," James said. "Mr. Griswold hasn't told us anything at all."

"Maybe we should start in a different room," Nisha said. "Somewhere nobody is looking."

"I agree," Matthew spoke up. "If you follow what everyone else is doing, you'll always come in behind. Have any of you noticed that the clock—"

"But we *know* there are three puzzles in this room," Emily interjected. Her brother frowned, she assumed because she was disagreeing with him, but she continued with what she wanted to say. "We might waste time wandering aimlessly, when we could find and solve something right here."

"We don't even know what to look for," Maddie complained. "A 'puzzle' could be all sorts of things. It's not like Mr. Griswold laid out jigsaw puzzles to solve."

"I found one!" a voice called across the room, and the slowly churning blender turned on high as everyone ran toward a table in the corner, which quickly became surrounded. Emily and her friends ended up on the outskirts.

"See?" Matthew said. "This is what happens to followers."

"We're here. We might as well see what the fuss is about." Nisha slid her backpack to the floor and thrust her notebook toward James. "Hold this. I'm small; I'm going in."

Before anyone could stop her, she dove under the armpits of the people in front of them and disappeared.

"Can you see anything?" Emily asked her brother, the tallest in their group.

"No. Get on my shoulders." Matthew stooped down.

"You'll drop me."

Matthew rolled his eyes. "Geez, you don't trust me to do anything, do you?"

His words stung, and to prove him wrong, Emily flung one leg over his shoulder. James and Maddie helped balance her, and Matthew rose slowly.

"What do you see?" James said.

"Can you tell what it is?" Maddie asked.

"People are looking at something on the table. It's . . ." A view opened up, and Emily giggled when she realized what the group was working on.

"You can let me down," she said.

"What? What's so funny?" Her friends repeated the questions over one another.

Before Emily could reply, Nisha popped back out of the crowd. "It's a jigsaw puzzle," she announced.

Maddie groaned. "Are you kidding me? He really *did* lay out jigsaw puzzles?"

"One, at least," Emily said, nodding to confirm Nisha's report.

"A jigsaw puzzle can take a long time to put together," Matthew said.

"Not to mention we can't even get to it," James added.

"And we don't know if it's one of the four puzzles Errol Roy said we'd need to find for the solution," Maddie said. "Matthew's right. We need to start somewhere else." She nudged Emily. "You're the Book Scavenger brains of our group. Where do you think we should start?"

"Well, maybe we could . . ." The truth was that Emily had no idea. She might know Book Scavenger well, and Mr. Griswold might have created both that game and this one, but she felt totally at a loss for what to do next. On Book Scavenger it was clear: There was a map, you picked either a book you wanted to find or a location near you with a hidden book, the clue was then provided, you solved it, and bam! A simple series of steps to follow.

But with Unlock the Rock there were no steps outlined for them. All she knew—all *anyone* knew—was that the goal involved finding an escaped prisoner using four puzzles hidden somewhere on Alcatraz.

"I know where we can start," Matthew said. "I found another puzzle."

CHAPTER 20

"H AVE ANY OF YOU noticed the clock in this room isn't working?" Matthew asked.

Everyone turned and Matthew hissed, "Don't all look at once or you'll tip everyone else off!"

"The one outside the dining hall wasn't working, either," Emily remembered.

Matthew nodded. "It was stopped at two forty and this one is stopped at eight twenty. It might be a coincidence, but if we find another clock and it's also stopped, then maybe—"

"They're part of a coded message?" James said.

Emily was simultaneously impressed with her brother and disappointed in herself for missing what he'd noticed. When Matthew had pointed out that first broken clock, she hadn't considered it to be anything more than what it appeared.

"Let's go on a clock hunt!" James said.

"I'll keep track of the different times," Nisha volunteered, holding her sketchbook in the crook of her arm.

"Write down the location for each one," Maddie said, "in case the numbers need to be put in a certain order."

They made their way to the dining hall exit, keeping an eye out for more clocks as they went. Emily noticed people subtly (and not so subtly) nudging one another as she and her friends passed. When they had been listening to Mr. Griswold and Errol Roy explain how Unlock the Rock would be played, Emily had felt for a moment like a regular player in a regular game. She loved being in that mind-set of narrowed concentration on a task and thinking about game strategy. She'd forgotten all about the threatening notes that had been tucked into her locker and backpack, and the gossip on the Book Scavenger forums that pegged her as the player to beat. Knowing that someone in this crowd wanted her out of the game was worrying, but it annoyed her, too.

What kind of person would want to win a game by intimidating a competitor out of playing? How satisfying would it actually be to win that way? It seemed like winning by default, to Emily. You'd always know deep down you didn't deserve it, even if you pretended otherwise. It would be like flipping to the back of a puzzle magazine for the answer before you'd even given the puzzle a chance.

It especially bothered her that she'd let the person's scare tactics chip away at her own confidence. Not to mention, if a competitor fixated on Emily and her friends, assuming they had an advantage, there were other contestants who'd fly under their radar. Contestants who might be even better competitors, like Mr. Quisling, Miss Linden, Bookacuda, and plenty more people at this event.

"There's another clock." Nisha quietly indicated one hanging just before the exit to the dining hall and next to an old, peeling staircase that was roped off. This clock also wasn't working, and it looked brand-new and very out-of-place, which made it seem likely Matthew was onto something.

"What about up here?" James asked, leaning into the staircase to look up. A cord ran from the rusted pipe handrail to the opposing wall, dangling a sign that said AUTHORIZED PERSONNEL ONLY. A woman wearing the SECURITY jacket approached them.

"That upstairs area isn't part of the game," she said, so they left the dining hall and continued their hunt for more clocks.

The main area of the prison had four blocks of cells. Emily and her friends wanted to do a thorough check, so they ran to one end to start. They walked through a doorway with a sign overhead that said D-BLOCK, and it felt like the temperature dropped ten degrees. D-Block was a long room with three tiers of jail cells facing a wall of windows that looked out to the water. From here the view was misty and gray, with bits of the San Francisco skyline visible in the distance.

The towering wall of cages was a lot to take in, and for a moment they all stood silently. At the opposite end of the long room, a park ranger's voice echoed in the lofty space. He seemed to be talking to himself about Alcatraz history.

". . . this segregation unit was used for prisoners with behavioral problems. One of Alcatraz's most infamous and vicious inmates, the Birdman, spent much of his time in this section, segregated from the other prisoners. . . ."

There were no actors in these cells, and Emily stared up at the empty rows of small rooms, trying to imagine having to live in one day after day. Did that experience help the prisoners who had behavioral problems get better, or not? she wondered.

"No blinds on the windows? It'd be miserable to sleep in here," Matthew said. "Not to mention freezing." He tucked his fists under his armpits.

"The prisoners had a nice view on a clear day," James pointed out.

"Is that better or worse," Nisha pondered, "to constantly see a beautiful outside world, but know you can't participate in it?"

"Worse," Maddie said. "You're always reminded of what you don't have."

"I think it'd be better," Nisha said, "like a real-life vision board. It would help me stay hopeful that I'd be out there again someday."

Footsteps thundered into the room, and Emily and her friends whirled around to find three kids skidding to a stop.

"Did you find something, Surly Wombat?" one of them asked, looking from Emily to James and back. The other two giggled.

Maddie groaned. "You two attract too much attention."

At the opposite end, an older couple Emily hadn't realized were also in D-Block exited a cell near the ranger. It turned out he hadn't been talking to himself. The couple thanked the ranger and left through the door on the far side of the room.

"There's a puzzle at that end!" one of the kids cried, and they sprinted to the park ranger, their sneakers slapping down the cement hall. They disappeared inside the cell the couple had exited.

"Should we go see what's in there?" James asked.

"It feels more organized to stick with the clocks, instead of jumping around," Nisha said.

"Focus on the task at hand, don't worry about all the possible outcomes," Emily agreed, paraphrasing the woman who'd worked on the cube puzzle with their group.

"It's going to take us forever to find every clock, and we don't even know if they'll end up meaning anything," Maddie complained.

"Nobody's begging you to stick around," James said.

"You don't have to work with us if you want to do things a different way."

Maddie stiffened at that, but Nisha gently tugged on her arm. "We want you to stay," she said.

"Let's check this area for clocks, and when we get to that end we'll look at the puzzle, since we're already here," Matthew said.

His compromise made sense to everyone, and they got to work seeking out clocks.

In case another contestant happened by, they worked out a system where Emily and James walked past any clock they spotted but feigned interest in something else. Meanwhile, Nisha stood with her back to the clock while Matthew or Maddie surreptitiously checked the time and told her what to write down.

There were four clocks in D-Block, all of them broken. Two were stopped at the same time: one hung between the giant windows looking out to the bay and another was inside a jail cell. Both were stuck at 2:40, which seemed odd, but they decided to make note of both just in case the duplication mattered.

Loud whooping drew their attention to the far end, and the group of three kids came hopping out of a cell shouting, "We did it!" One of them called over to Emily, "Hey, Surly Wombat—have you done that puzzle yet?"

"No," she answered.

"We beat Surly Wombat to a puzzle!" The kids howled with excitement and left D-Block, celebrating.

Matthew clapped a hand on Emily's shoulder. "Ignore them. They're being stupid."

"I know. They didn't bother me." She really meant that, too, she realized—she wasn't just being defensive—but she also appreciated her brother looking out for her, so she added, "Thanks, though."

It actually struck Emily as funny, in a ridiculous way, that those kids would celebrate solving a puzzle before she did. Thinking about it made her realize that it was the challenge she was passionate about, the actual figuring out of a problem, not winning or being first. Not that she'd complain if she solved the game and won the prizes.

"Let's see what they found," she said.

The cell was one of six in a row used for solitary confinement. Each one had a solid steel door that could shut over the regular barred door. Everyone stepped inside the cell that contained a puzzle except for Nisha, who refused. She stood next to the park ranger instead, hugging her notebook to her chest.

If Emily couldn't imagine having to live in one of the other D-Block cells for a long period of time, she *really* couldn't imagine being in solitary confinement. If that steel door were closed, they'd be in total darkness. It smelled like wet rocks and was so cold, her fleece jacket felt as thin as a T-shirt. She'd probably hyperventilate if she were confined in the space for twenty minutes, let alone for days. She knew the men who stayed at Alcatraz were considered some of the worst criminals, but she didn't understand how being locked in a room like this would help them change for the better. She hoped they at least had been allowed a book and some reading time.

In the dim light of the cell, they could make out large circles stuck to the cement floor, arranged in the shape of a triangle.

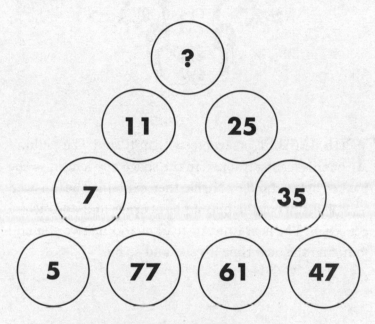

"It's a math puzzle," James said.

They contemplated in silence. Emily squinted and muttered the numbers out loud to help her focus on the problem and not get distracted by feeling that the darkness of the cell was closing in on her. Soon she spotted the pattern and shouted, "I've got it!"

CHAPTER 21

"THE ANSWER is seventeen," Emily said. She couldn't handle feeling trapped in the space any longer, so she backed out to stand by Nisha, then explained her answer.

"You start at the bottom left corner and add two to get seven. The next time, instead of adding two you add four, and the next time it's six, and so on."

$$5 + 2 = 7$$
$$7 + 4 = 11$$
$$11 + 6 = 17$$
$$17 + 8 = 25$$
$$25 + 10 = 35$$
$$35 + 12 = 47$$
$$47 + 14 = 61$$
$$61 + 16 = 77$$

"The number you add goes up by two each time," she said.

"So . . ." Still inside the cell, Matthew stared at the dots on the floor. "Is something supposed to happen?"

"You mean like confetti cannons exploding in celebration?" Maddie asked.

"No, but that would be a nice touch," Matthew replied.

James turned to the park ranger. "Do you know what we do next? Are we supposed to tell you the answer?"

The ranger shrugged. "I'm here to answer any questions you might have about Alcatraz, but I don't know anything about the puzzles. However, if you want to know more about how this island's history goes back well before the federal prison, even well before the Civil War when Alcatraz was a military outpost, to the original inhabitants of this area—the Ohlone and Coast Miwok peoples, who initially lived throughout the Bay Area—then I'm your guy."

Maddie had already opened the door to the next room. "Okay, we'll keep that in mind," she said, waving everyone through. "If we want to help Hollister get that money, we've got to keep moving."

That reminder was all the prodding Emily needed. Their group filed out the door to the D-Block and into the next space. "Maybe what we do with the seventeen will become clear once we solve more puzz . . ." Emily's voice trailed off as she took in their surroundings. The windows in this soaring three-story room were ablaze from the setting sun. Peach light washed over the cold concrete walls. But what really caught her breath were the books.

Underneath the windows, shelves lined the room, squeezed full with colorful spines. A quick glance at some of the titles—the Harry Potter series, *The Book Thief*, *Greenglass House*, *Seabiscuit*, and two rows full of Errol Roy's books—signaled this was set up for Garrison Griswold's game and not part of the historical prison tour, because most, if not all, of these books had been published after the prison closed in 1963. Emily stroked the book spines, and she started to browse. She couldn't help it—it was like they entranced her in a spell, which was broken when Nisha nearly shouted, "There's a clock!" Then she clapped a hand over her own mouth, remembering they were trying to be discreet.

In an attempt to cover Nisha's goof, Maddie intoned like a robot, "That clock is broken. How are we ever going to know what time it is?"

"It's almost six." At the sound of Mr. Quisling's voice, Emily looked up. She'd been so transfixed by the books, she hadn't realized he and Miss Linden were in the room. Two college-aged guys were also there, browsing books on the shelf, and the young girl, Iris, whom Emily had seen at Grace Cathedral and earlier on the ferry with her grandfather, passed through to enter D-Block the way Emily and her friends had come out.

"Hurry, Papa, hurry!" Iris said, tugging the older man's gloved hand. He exchanged a smile with Mr. Quisling and Miss Linden and rolled his eyes in a good-humored way.

"No wonder I'm starving," Matthew said. "We should take a break for food."

"We don't want to run out of time to get Hollister's store that money. Didn't you bring Goldfish crackers?" Emily reminded her brother.

"You won't have to take a break if you order the roast beef sandwich." Miss Linden winked.

Emily and her friends turned to each other with wide eyes. "There are puzzles with the food!" James said.

"Of course, Mr. Griswold would think of that." Emily shook her head. Hollister hadn't been exaggerating when he said there were puzzles and clues to be found everywhere. She wondered how many other puzzle opportunities they'd walked right by.

"One puzzle at a time, remember?" James said. "Let's finish what we're working on first."

"And what *are* you working on?" Miss Linden asked in a teasing tone.

"Oh no, you're not tricking us into revealing what we know," Maddie said.

Nisha had already written down the time of the first clock she'd spotted while they talked, shielding her notebook from the view of others. Behind Mr. Quisling's and Miss Linden's backs, Matthew directed Nisha's attention to another clock, an old cuckoo, sitting on top of a bookcase.

"Well, I'm glad *someone* is focused on the task at

hand," Miss Linden said. "Your teacher has been, uh, a little distracted."

"I'm not distracted. I'm observant."

Miss Linden grabbed Mr. Quisling's hands and wobbled his arms. "Come on, sourpuss. Let's get in the spirit of the game! Don't you want a year of books? And a bookshelf of honor in Hollister's store? We could call it Quisling's Corner. That has a nice ring."

Their teacher grunted in response. Miss Linden placed her hands on her hips and turned to survey the library. Her long black hair was threaded with pink and pulled forward over one shoulder. A hint of the tattoos that paraded up and down her right arm was visible above the collar of her fleece pullover.

"There must be a puzzle in this room, Brian. Probably more than one. Help me out here: If you were going to hide a message using books in a library, how might you go about doing that?"

Without hesitation Mr. Quisling tonelessly recited, "Arrange books in alphabetical order and place a book with the puzzle inside in the wrong section. Use book titles to form a message and group those together, surrounded by other titles to help conceal them. Arrange books to form a message in Morse code by using tall books as a substitute for dashes and short books as a substitute for dots."

"Oh, wow . . ." Emily said. She felt like she was seeing the room now with puzzle vision.

"There we go. Now he's coming back to us." Miss

Linden squeezed his shoulders encouragingly, like a trainer getting a boxer psyched to go in a ring.

Mr. Quisling couldn't help but smile. Her pep seemed to be wearing down his resolve to be serious.

"You're a fan of Errol Roy's just like James, aren't you, Mr. Quisling?" Maddie asked. "Did you think he'd be here, or were you surprised?"

Their teacher nodded. "I am a fan, yes. And I was very surprised."

"Shocked is more like it." Miss Linden gave him a playful bump with her hip. "That's why he's so distracted. We've been on a mission to find him—Errol Roy—more so than to find puzzles."

Mr. Quisling frowned. "I'm not trying to *find* him, not like a groupie or anything, anyway. I just thought there was something . . . peculiar about him being here. I want to observe him more, that's all."

"You too?" James asked.

"What do you mean 'you too'?" Emily asked.

"I also thought it was weird, seeing him." James had a distant look on his face, like he was watching the moment replay in his imagination. "At first I thought it was because he looked different than I had expected. But he was so uncomfortable talking to us. I don't get why he came. Nobody would have expected him to, so why bother if it's going to make you that uncomfortable?"

Miss Linden nodded sympathetically. "It can be disappointing if a role model doesn't live up to how we imagine them to be, can't it? But Errol Roy must be in his eighties, and sometimes when people get to that age, they feel the pressure of time running out. Maybe he's regretted his reclusive life or felt like he owed an appearance to you and his other readers, but the reality of being here, in front of a crowd, was too much for him."

"One thing's for sure," Mr. Quisling said. "You kids should enjoy your time playing the game."

Miss Linden hooked her arm through Mr. Quisling's. "Yes, we won't take you away from it any longer. The clock's ticking!"

Emily and her friends exchanged a look, unsure if Miss Linden's phrase was a signal that she knew about the puzzle they were working on. The teacher and librarian moved on to D-Block.

"Let's hurry and find the rest of the clocks," James said.

Emily's friends exited the library through the passageway that led back to the main cellblock room, but she couldn't resist lingering. It was hard to shake off Mr. Quisling's list of puzzle possibilities hidden among the library books. Familiar bold lettering caught Emily's eye. *The Twain Conspiracy* by Lucy Leonard. Seeing the book gave her that feeling of being on the verge of remembering something you forgot you were trying to remember.

She pulled the book from the shelf and opened the back cover to look at the author photo. Lucy Leonard's hair was more sleek and styled, and she wore a lot of makeup, but without the red-framed glasses she'd had on at the event Emily made the connection. There was no denying it:

The woman in the photo was the same woman who had helped them solve the puzzle on the pier.

Lucy Leonard was playing Unlock the Rock?

CHAPTER 22

MATTHEW POKED his head back in the library. "You coming?" he asked.

Emily followed him out but couldn't stop thinking about Lucy Leonard playing Unlock the Rock. Her mom would flip out when she told her. Did this mean Lucy Leonard was also an avid Book Scavenger player?

Walking down the middle corridor, which was called Broadway, they passed the cell Emily had seen when they'd first entered, where a prisoner was reading a book. Matthew leaned against the bars and asked, "Hey, guy, do you know what time it is?"

"Matthew." Emily tugged at her brother's arm. "Don't give away what we're doing."

A family of two women with a young boy and girl huddled outside the cell of the guitar-strumming prisoner, who was farther down the aisle. The boy knelt on the floor, writing something on paper, and his family members concentrated on what he was doing. Emily didn't think they had heard Matthew's question, but she still felt pressure to keep the puzzle they were working on a secret in addition to working as fast as possible.

The reading prisoner ignored her brother. Matthew bent to get a look at the cover. "*A Swiftly Tilting Planet*," he read aloud. "Any good?"

Emily sighed and continued walking with James, Maddie, and Nisha. Why spend your time doing Unlock the Rock if you weren't going to take it seriously?

The prisoner gave in this time and answered Matthew. "Pretty good. Chapter seven is my favorite."

"Matthew, you're not being funny," she called to him. "Stop wasting time."

Her brother frowned and jogged up to their group. One of the moms outside the musician's cell shouted, "You got it!" The little girl replied, "We solved it?!" She jumped up and squealed, and the foursome ran off. Emily studied the cell when they walked by, but there was only the prisoner, his guitar, and sheet music scattered next to him on the cot—nothing that looked like a puzzle.

There was also no clock in the cell, and it was a relief to know the other group hadn't been working on the same thing as them.

"We're spending too much time on this one puzzle," Maddie chided their group. "We need to hurry."

They found three more stopped clocks along the Broadway corridor, and four more on the next one over, Michigan Avenue. When they reached A-Block, they were met with a taut wall of plastic sheeting that ran all the way from the cement floor to the third-story ceiling, which kept them from going farther. Dim light illuminated the plastic, revealing bars of scaffolding behind. A sheet of plywood with a wooden latch to keep it closed served as a makeshift door, with caution tape stretched across the barrier on either side, like a belt.

"What's through there?" James extended a hand toward the latch.

An Alcatraz park ranger barked at them, like she was about to prevent them from stepping off a cliff, "That area's under reconstruction!"

The ranger was only as tall as Emily, although her Smokey Bear–style hat added several inches, and she wore very large, very thick glasses that obscured most of her face.

"Sorry," James said. "We weren't sure if it was part of the game."

"I've heard that one before," the ranger said. "And no, I can't let you take a quick look around, no matter how careful you might be."

Emily and her friends exchanged confused looks. They had no interest in going back there if it wasn't part of the game.

"Shame it's closed off, though. It's a fascinating part of Alcatraz's history." The woman clasped her hands in front of herself and rocked back on her heels. "It's the only part of this building that dates back to the original military prison that was here on Alcatraz, before the maximum-security prison everyone knows it for today. And, of course, the dungeon's also back there. That's what most everyone is curious about."

"Dungeon!?" Nisha said, stepping closer to Maddie.

"I told you the dungeon existed," James said.

"Come on," Emily said. "We need to find the rest of the"—she looked to the ranger, unsure whether she could trust her—"puzzles."

The ranger saluted them and continued on her rounds. "Good luck!" she called.

After walking through the dining hall, library, and all the cellblocks they could access, they had found sixteen clocks, all stopped at a variety of times. There wasn't a pattern they could discern yet, but there were three areas left to check: the chapel room upstairs, the shower room downstairs, and the administrative offices. They decided to split up in order to be as speedy as possible. Nisha, Maddie, and James went off to check the chapel and shower room, while Emily and Matthew headed for the administrative offices.

On their way, they nearly bumped into Bookacuda walking out of the dining hall with his two friends behind him. They must have had something to eat, because the boy with the curly mop of hair had a little red sauce on his chin, and Bookacuda had a toothpick sticking from the side of his mouth, like he'd just finished a meal. The girl in their trio had a map of Alcatraz open, which she folded into a small rectangle as soon as she saw them.

"Hey, Swamp Bat," Bookacuda said. The toothpick bobbed up and down, and Emily imagined he thought it made him look tough, but more than anything it reminded her of a goat chewing on a piece of straw. "I think I've nearly got the solution. You?"

"Ignore him," Emily said, as much to herself as to her brother.

Replying under his breath, Matthew said, "Why ignore him when we can do this?" Before Emily could say another word, her brother darted to a staircase just past Bookacuda. He called over his shoulder, "Hurry, Em! We want to get to it before they do." He disappeared down the stairs.

"Matthew!" She had no idea what in the world her brother was thinking, and they were wasting time on Bookacuda when they needed to finish their clock hunt.

"There's nothing down there. We've already looked." Bookacuda seemed uncertain, though, exchanging looks with his two friends, who nodded their agreement. Even though Emily was irritated with her brother's antics, she was more fed up with Bookacuda's know-it-all tone.

"Are you sure?" she asked. "How do you know new puzzles don't get laid out as the game goes on?"

His eyebrows popped up at the thought. Emily had tossed out the theory spontaneously—the question hadn't occurred to her until just that moment—and now even she was wondering, *How do I know that's not what happens?*

"Solved it!" Matthew's voice carried upstairs.

"Solved what?" Bookacuda said the exact words Emily was thinking.

Bookacuda got to the stairwell first with Emily behind him. Bookacuda's friends half-heartedly followed. When they reached the lower level, Emily could see over Bookacuda's shoulder to Goldfish crackers that had been laid out on the cement floor in the shape of the number 165.

"What does that mean?" Bookacuda asked. "Is that the solution or the puzzle?"

"I'm not saying." Matthew hiked up the stairs with Emily, leaving Bookacuda pacing around the Goldfish and attempting to figure out the problem.

"Stop gaping and help me!" Bookacuda snapped at his partners, who hadn't moved from the stairs.

Once they were back on the main level and out of earshot, Emily asked her brother, "What does 165 mean?"

Matthew shrugged. "It was the first thing that popped in my head." He grinned at Emily. "And you thought my snacks were a waste of space."

CHAPTER

23

THE ADMINISTRATION WING consisted of offices and the visiting room, where the friends and family of Alcatraz prisoners had sat to speak to the inmates through a small square window. Emily and Matthew ducked into the visiting room first, but it was packed with contestants, probably because a lot of people were waiting for a chance to talk with the actors playing a prisoner and a visitor sitting on either side of the glass.

The siblings bumped against other contestants as they inspected the small room and found one broken clock. There was a player scanning a magnifying glass along a narrow, horizontal window that was nearly at Matthew's eye level, enlarging tiny symbols.

Emily added that to her mental list of other potential puzzles they could return to in the event their clocks didn't amount to anything, but it was getting difficult to keep track. She should have been writing these down in her Book Scavenger notebook.

They made their way to the main administration space. This area was bigger, so it didn't feel as crowded, but plenty of contestants meandered about. Emily and Matthew peered through panes of glass into a control room that had been set up like a museum display. Two more clocks were spotted amid the old-fashioned technology and communication devices: bulky boxes covered in dials and switches, a tabletop microphone, a typewriter on a metal desk, and three of those phones with curly cords.

They turned quickly from the control room, eager to move on, but Matthew smacked straight into Lucy Leonard, who had stepped in from outside.

"You!" Emily jumped back in surprise. The woman froze, looking like she'd been caught red-handed. Outside the doorway behind her, lampposts glowed in the violet fog of dusk.

"I know who you are," Emily blurted out.

Lucy Leonard shifted her weight from foot to foot, like she was eager to keep moving, but at Emily's words she gave a tentative smile.

"Who am I?" she asked.

"You wrote *The Twain Conspiracy*. Our mom is a huge fan."

"No way!" Matthew said. "You're that same lady from the theater? You look a lot different up close. My sister's not kidding, either—our mom really is a huge fan. She dragged us to hear you talk the other—"

"Matthew!" Emily thwapped her brother. *Dragged* made it sound like they hadn't been interested in going, which was true, but he didn't need to tell the author that.

"Well, it's great to know your mom is a fan. Make sure to tell her I said thank you for reading my book." Lucy Leonard smiled. "Now, those puzzles aren't going to find themselves, right?" With a small wave, she darted away.

A question popped into Emily's mind. "Ms. Leonard," she called after her. "What's your username?"

Lucy stopped and turned. "My what?"

"For Book Scavenger. What's your username?"

"It's, uh . . ." She scrunched up her face, appearing perplexed by the question. "I don't have one." She gave another wave and was off.

Emily stared after her, frowning. Matthew poked her shoulder. "There's more to the administration area that way," he said, pointing through a doorway.

"Okay . . . ," Emily said absentmindedly.

You didn't *have* to be an avid Book Scavenger player to be here for Unlock the Rock. It was possible to register for the event on the website and do nothing else, although the majority of people here probably played Book Scavenger, or at least were fans of Mr. Griswold's games. There was something in the way Lucy Leonard was approaching Unlock the Rock that seemed so odd, so different from everyone else. She was here by herself and working solo, it seemed, and her approach with the block puzzle when she'd joined their team on the pier had been pretty laid-back. It almost didn't seem like she was that interested in playing the game, but then why else would she be here?

"Emily." Her brother's voice drifted over from a nearby room.

Emily followed the sound and found him inside an office sparsely furnished with a plain table, two chairs, a watercooler in the corner, a bench, and an old-fashioned Coca-Cola chest. Folded over the back of one of the chairs was a gray raincoat.

A big window looked outside to the lighthouse. This office also had the same interior window that closed it off but made it possible for Alcatraz visitors to view the inside.

"Are we allowed in here?" Emily asked.

"The door was ajar," Matthew said.

"Matthew, we don't have time to waste." If the puzzle they were trying to piece together and solve ended up being a dead end, they would need time to find the correct ones for Roy's solution. "There aren't any clocks in here. Let's go."

"Wait—look at what's on this desk."

On the tabletop there was a set of keys, a typed sheet of paper, and an envelope. Matthew picked up the paper and held it out to Emily. "This is the sheet Mr. Roy read from to start the game."

"What are you doing?" Emily asked. "Don't mess with his stuff."

"How do you know this isn't part of the game? Remember how James and Mr. Quisling said something seemed off about him? It got me thinking that maybe he was acting. Maybe we're *supposed* to find these things."

Emily bit the inside of her lip, considering this. To her, Errol Roy had seemed genuinely anxious. If his stage fright had been an act, then he deserved an Academy Award.

"You do what you want," she finally said. "I'm checking the rest of the area for clocks."

She left Matthew behind in the office with the Coca-Cola chest and walked through a doorway labeled WARDEN'S OFFICE. Several other teams were searching for puzzles and scrutinizing various details. One group seemed to think the framed images hung on the wall made up a rebus puzzle, and a duo was figuring out a math problem similar to the one Emily's group had solved in solitary confinement. This one used small wooden blocks set up in a pyramid.

Emily finished checking the administrative offices and added two more broken clocks to their list. She was making note of the time and location in her Book Scavenger notebook when a man roared from back down the hall, "What do you think you're doing?!"

CHAPTER 24

EMILY RAN BACK into the room where she'd left her brother. Matthew had his back to the desk and his hands up as he faced Errol Roy.

"Were you going through my coat?" Mr. Roy's skin flushed purple, visible even through his wispy, long white hair and beard.

"I thought—"

"No, you didn't. That's exactly what you *didn't* do. *Think.*"

Emily wasn't the only one who came running at the sound of shouting. A crowd gathered outside the glass windows. Fiona's mother pushed her way into the room with Fiona right behind. "Is everything all right, Mr. Roy?" Mrs. Duncan asked. She stood next to Roy, and Fiona wedged in between her mom and Matthew. It felt as if everyone were positioning themselves against her brother, so Emily stood close to his side.

Mr. Roy was shaking, clearly still angry, but he was also taking in the faces of contestants staring through the windows of the room, and Mrs. Duncan's head tilted with concern.

"I'm fine," he said, his voice lowered to a normal volume. "This hoodlum was going through my things."

"Oh my!" Mrs. Duncan pressed a hand to her neck. "Did he steal from you?"

"No!" Matthew insisted. "And I wasn't going through his things."

"A lot of things have gone missing today," Fiona piped up. "Someone also stole my charm bracelet."

"Your bracelet fell off on the ferry," Emily snapped.

Fiona's eyes widened, all innocence and *poor me*. "Well, I *thought* it fell off. I never found it, so I don't know for sure."

Maddie, Nisha, and James appeared, squeezing between the onlookers clogging the entrance to the room.

"What's going on?" Maddie asked.

Mr. Roy sagged into the chair. "Can everyone please leave now?" He tugged at the collar of his sweatshirt, flapping it open and closed as if to cool himself off. The room was getting quite crowded.

"Let's give the man some space while we get to the bottom of this," Mrs. Duncan said.

"There's nothing to get to the bottom of," Matthew insisted.

Fiona acted like a security guard, trying to guide

everyone back from Mr. Roy in the chair, but Matthew shrugged her off.

"Bug off!" he said.

"Is everything all right?" Mr. Griswold's voice called out, and soon he came into the room. Everyone shifted and bumped against one another to make space as he scooted sideways between Emily and Matthew to stand next to Errol Roy.

"There's a thief among us, Mr. Griswold!" Fiona said.

"I knew there was a thief," Maddie crowed. "My backpack was stolen earlier."

"Jack found your backpack," Emily corrected Maddie. "It wasn't stolen."

"We need to find out what happened," Fiona's mother said.

"Is everything all right, Errol? Are you okay?" Mr. Griswold asked.

Mr. Roy's head was in his hand. "I'm fine. Everything's fine. I'd like to be left alone."

"Everything is most certainly *not* fine," Mrs. Duncan sniffed. "Mr. Roy caught this young man red-handed stealing from him."

"No, he didn't!" Matthew gripped the straps of his backpack so tightly his knuckles whitened.

Errol Roy looked up sharply. "I never said that."

Maddie sized Matthew up. "You *were* right next to me after the tram crashed and my backpack went missing."

Matthew rolled his eyes. "Go look for Scooby snacks, Velma."

Mr. Griswold held up his hands. "All right, let's just—"

"That's right!" Fiona wedged herself onto Matthew's other side. They stood eye to eye, but her curly hair gave her extra height. She tipped a finger toward Matthew's nose. "You were the kid next to me on the ferry at the exact moment my bracelet went missing."

Matthew winced, which Emily thought had more to do with being called a kid by Fiona, but the wince read like he'd been caught in a lie.

"You can't say it was the exact moment," Emily argued. "You don't know when you lost it."

"When it was *taken*," Fiona corrected.

"Seriously?!" Matthew tugged on his green-sprout hair, and his elbows bumped both Maddie and Fiona away from him. "I. Didn't. Take. Anything! From you or anyone else. This is nuts." He turned to Emily. "You've been with me the entire day. Tell them."

Emily felt like she was trapped in an elevator with eight people crammed in that room around Errol Roy. For the first time that evening, the frigid prison was feeling warm, uncomfortably warm even with all eyes on her.

She hadn't been in the room when Roy confronted her brother, but if Matthew had been going through his coat, she was certain he thought it was a prop in the game, as he'd said. Emily knew her brother wouldn't steal. The same items Emily had seen when she'd been in the room before were still there: the set of keys, the letter Roy had read from, an envelope—

"I can't believe you," Matthew said. Emily realized he had misread her hesitation as doubt about his innocence. "I wouldn't steal." He shook his head. "I thought you knew me better than that."

"No, I didn't—" Emily waved her hands, trying to grab back the minute she'd been lost in thought so she could speak up firmly in defense of her brother.

Matthew slid his backpack off his shoulders and offered it to Mr. Griswold. "I've been with Emily and her friends this entire afternoon, so if I really was a thief, I'd have the bracelet on me, right? Here. Go through my stuff. You'll see."

"Matthew, I'm not accusing you—" Mr. Griswold's eyes were soft and kind, but her brother was angry and determined to defend himself.

"I'll show you myself." Matthew yanked the zipper open and pulled out the empty bag of Goldfish, his flashlight, a calculator . . . He slammed all the contents of his bag, one by one, on the desk next to Mr. Roy's things. Emily knew her brother, and she could tell this wasn't a show or an act—he was genuinely upset.

"See? That's everything. None of it is yours, Maddie—or Fiona's or Mr. Roy's."

Fiona shrugged, not impressed. "You could have put my bracelet in a pocket."

Matthew shoved his hands in his pocket and jerked to a stop, like it had been filled with jam. He drew his hand back out. A charm bracelet dangled from his fingers.

CHAPTER

25

"I KNEW IT!" Fiona shouted. She plucked the bracelet free. For once Matthew was stunned into silence, and Emily was stumped, too. How could that be? She absolutely believed her brother wasn't the thief.

But how would a missing bracelet have ended up in his pocket if he hadn't put it there?

"Shame on you," Fiona's mother said to Matthew. She elbowed her way in front of Fiona and refastened the bracelet on her daughter's extended wrist, at the same time snapping at Mr. Griswold, "Are you going to just stand there—"

"Ma'am, I'm sure there's—"

"Or are you going to do something?"

"Matthew wouldn't—"

"Oh, but he did! The proof was in his pocket," Mrs. Duncan said.

"I didn't take anything—" Matthew tried to interject, but Fiona's mother continued.

"He should be kicked out of the game—and perhaps his whole group of friends as well! After all, how do we know he acted alone?"

"I wasn't a part of it," Maddie spoke up. "I've been a victim as well."

"Oh, please," Emily muttered.

Maddie's face flushed and she stood ramrod straight. "You know what? I don't need this." She spun around, pushed past James and Nisha, and left the room.

"Maddie," Nisha called after her weakly, but Maddie continued to nudge past the other contestants until she was out of sight.

Emily was too annoyed with Maddie for attacking her brother and being so dramatic about her backpack to feel anything other than *good riddance*.

"All right, everybody, calm down," Mr. Griswold said. "Matthew, why don't you come with me? We can talk about this elsewhere. Privately," he added when Fiona's mother tried to follow.

Emily helped her brother collect his strewn items and put them back into his backpack. "You know I didn't take that bracelet, right?" he asked, fixing her with a piercing stare, reading the nagging question written across her face: *How did it get in your pocket?*

But she said, "I believe you, Matthew."

He nodded and walked out behind Mr. Griswold.

With Matthew talking to Mr. Griswold, and Maddie having stalked off, it was down to Emily, James, and Nisha to figure out the clocks. They regrouped in the dining hall and sat at an empty table next to the gruff prisoner who'd mugged a face at Mr. Griswold when the game had kicked off in this same room well over an hour ago. The prisoner looked up from his chili-filled bread bowl and growled at the trio like a territorial dog.

Emily might have laughed or played along with a yelp earlier in the evening, but now she didn't even crack a smile. She didn't much feel in the spirit of the game anymore. The prison itself was unrelentingly dour, with a chill that filtered through her clothes. If this was a regular Book Scavenger hunt, she'd say *forget it* and go home, but they were trapped on the island until time ran out.

"He's so cranky," James said forlornly, to nobody in particular. He was talking about Errol Roy. His impression of his beloved author had only gone further downhill after Roy's dispute with Matthew.

Nisha was the only one of the three who appeared to have retained a chipper and determined resolve. Her notebook was open on the table to the twenty-one clocks she'd drawn.

"What do you think? What could they mean?" she

asked, trying to draw their focus back to the task at hand.

James sighed heavily, but leaned closer to scrutinize the pictures. Emily stared at a water stain on the ceiling: an enormous brown ring the size of a bathtub. Being at Alcatraz to play the game had sounded like an exciting idea in the beginning, but now everything seemed to be falling apart, both the old prison and the game. There was the plaster peeling off the walls like a day-old sunburn, and the belongings that had gone missing. The patches of chipped-away flooring all over the dining hall, and her brother accused of being a thief.

"What do you think Mr. Griswold is saying to Matthew?" Emily asked.

James looked up from the notebook. "Don't worry," he said. "Mr. Griswold knows your brother. He knows Matthew wouldn't have taken that bracelet."

James was probably right. It was likely Mr. Griswold wouldn't blame Matthew, but then the bracelet *had* been in his pocket. How did you account for that? The only explanation she could come up with was that someone was trying to frame her brother as a thief, but that was no comfort. Who would do that and why?

Emily eyed the other contestants scattered across the dining hall. Some were camped out at tables like their group; others were running in or running out, presumably on their way to find another puzzle. There was a line at the back food counter, and a group that had settled in around the jigsaw puzzle, laughing and eating snacks. Everyone seemed totally invested in the game, or at least invested in having fun, and everyone seemed immune to the setting, which was feeling more depressing to Emily by the minute.

Nisha adjusted her glasses. "I know you're worried about your brother, but he was the one who had the idea about the clocks as a code. I bet he'd be disappointed if our time here ends and we never figure out whether or not he was right, and what the code said."

She turned to James and said, "And I know you feel let down by Errol Roy, but you signed up for the game before you knew he'd be involved. Solve Errol Roy's mystery for Hollister, if you're no longer interested in doing it for yourself."

The three of them looked across the dining hall to where the bookseller stood chatting with Jack. Hollister must have felt their attention because he turned, his gaze eventually finding their group. He raised a thumb, which was reassuring somehow, even though Emily didn't know if the gesture was telling them he knew about Matthew's situation and everything was all right, or if he was encouraging them in the game, or if it was simply a way to say hello from a distance.

But the positive gesture connected with Emily. She could hear his voice calling out *FUN-raiser* at the Lucy Leonard event a couple of nights ago. If Hollister could persevere and be cheery despite nearly losing his business and sentimental items in a fire, then the three of them could certainly rally and at least attempt to solve Errol Roy's mystery.

"Okay," Emily said. "So what do we do with these clocks?"

D-BLOCK:

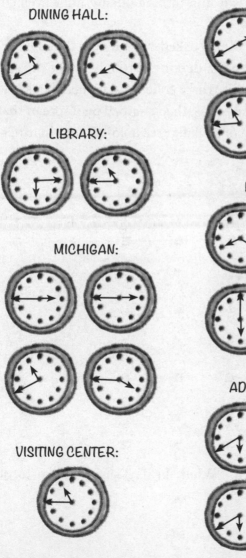

DINING HALL:

LIBRARY:

MICHIGAN:

VISITING CENTER:

BROADWAY:

ADMINISTRATION:

Nisha, James, and Maddie had only found working clocks in the chapel and the shower room, so Nisha kept those in a separate list, thinking they probably were normal clocks and not part of the code.

They stared silently at the drawings. Nisha turned her notebook this way and that. Suddenly James yelped, "Semaphore!"

"Semaphore?" Emily asked. "What does that mean?"

James was already digging through his backpack, and he pulled out his trusty codes and ciphers book. He flipped through the pages, then stopped on a spread that showed a diagram of stick figures holding flags in different positions.

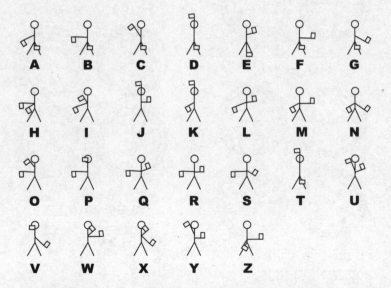

Nisha frowned. "What do flag signals have to do with time?"

"I get it," Emily said. "The flags are the hands of the clock. Is that what you're thinking?"

"Exactly," James said.

They set out assigning letters to each clock based on where the arms were stuck, but when they were done, they were left with a nonsensical list of letters:

DINING HALL:

I N

LIBRARY:

F O

MICHIGAN:

R R
I S

VISITING CENTER:

O

D-BLOCK:

L L
O W

BROADWAY:

N G
D L

ADMINISTRATION:

A N
A M

"So maybe they're not in order," Emily said.

They played around with the letters, trying to arrange them into a message, but quickly decided that would be futile.

"I have an idea." Emily unzipped her backpack and pulled out a binder that held a printout she'd brought of the prison floor plan. Using Nisha's notes, she wrote down the letter that corresponded to each clock in the spot where they had found it. At first this didn't seem to change anything, but then she turned the map on its side, and they realized the letters appeared to be laid out in four rows, and the top row formed the word *Follow*. Reading each line of the clock letters from left to right, they deciphered the message:

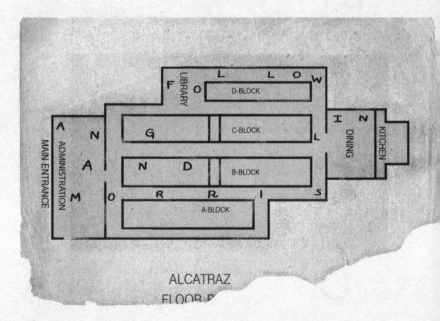

ALCATRAZ
FLOOR P

"'Follow Anglin and Morris,'" Nisha read aloud.

"Anglin and Morris?" Emily said. "What does that mean? Are those names?"

"They sound familiar," James said. "I feel like I should know this."

"Maybe we should ask an actor," Emily suggested. "Maybe there are two men here called Anglin and Morris, and if we can find them, they'll lead us where we're supposed to go."

James leaned toward the prisoner. "Excuse me, sir?"

The man was using a chunk of bread to scoop up a bite of his chili. He didn't even glance James's way.

James tried again, "Do you know Anglin and Morris?"

"The roast beef's the best thing on the menu," the man grumbled.

"Uh, okay . . . thanks." James turned back to their table.

"Don't give up yet," Nisha said. "Let's ask more of the actors and see what they say."

Two other prisoners were in the dining hall playing dominoes, but they continued their game like the kids weren't even there.

Emily and her friends entered the main room with all the cellblocks. None of the three prisoners who were in cells said a word when they were asked about Anglin and Morris.

"There's also the guard on the second level," James reminded them, but the stairs going up were roped off with a chain.

"Hello up there!" James called, and soon the guard appeared.

"Authorized personnel only," he said.

"Do you know where we can find Anglin and Morris?" Emily called up.

"Anglin and Morris?" the guard repeated. "You won't be able to find them. They're long gone. They escaped—didn't you hear?"

CHAPTER 26

"THAT'S WHY the names are familiar! I read about this," James said. "Those are the men who escaped Alcatraz and were never found."

"There was a cell that talked about that," Nisha said. "The one with the fake head on the pillow."

Nisha led the way to that cell, which seemed to be set up as it would have looked when the men had escaped. The cell had a few personal items—a coat hanging on a hook, a painting and a couple of books propped on the shelf, a notebook folded open with a doodle in it on the small table next to the cell bars. The ventilation grate under the sink had been removed and leaned against the back wall, to show that a hole the size of an encyclopedia had been dug through the concrete. A papier-mâché head rested on a pillow, tucked in under covers to look like a sleeping man.

"So Anglin and Morris were real people?" Emily asked.

"It was three people," Nisha said, reading a placard hung next to the cell. "The Anglin brothers, Clarence and John, and Frank Morris. All three escaped Alcatraz one night in 1962. They spent months digging tunnels through their cells with a spoon, and then one night they crawled through the holes they'd made, climbed up the utility corridor that's behind the cell, got on the roof, shimmied down a drainpipe, climbed over a barbed-wire fence, and then launched a raft they made out of raincoats into the bay. They were never found, and most people think they drowned trying to cross to land."

"They made a raft out of *raincoats*? What kind of Inspector Gadget sorcery is that?" James asked.

"They dug a tunnel with a spoon?" Emily said incredulously. "Man, they had a lot of patience. That must have taken forever."

She wished Matthew were with them. He'd have loved hearing this story.

"I think there's an old movie about this escape," Nisha said. "My grandpa mentioned one called *Escape from Alcatraz*, when he heard I'd be here for Unlock the Rock."

"So what do you think 'follow Anglin and Morris' is telling us to do?" James asked, bringing them back to the task at hand.

The question stumped them, until Emily paid closer attention to the doodle on the notebook.

WHAT IS IS WRONG WITH THIS PICTURE?

"Look!" Emily said. "Do you think that's a puzzle?"

Everyone huddled close to the bars, trying to get a good look at the picture. They each pointed out possibilities for what was wrong with the drawing.

"How many toes does the cat have?"

"Is the ear facing the right way?"

"Does the tail look more like a snake to you?"

"Wait!" Once Emily spotted the answer, she couldn't believe she hadn't noticed it right away. "The answer is *is*. The word *is* is repeated twice."

"Well, that's a trick," James said, disappointed.

"What does it mean?" Nisha asked. "What are we supposed to do with *is*?"

"Maybe it's not the word *is*, but an abbreviation for where we're supposed to go next?" Emily suggested.

Once again Emily removed her floor plan of the cell

house, but there wasn't a room in the building that correlated with *IS*.

"Mr. Griswold did say some puzzles might lead us outside," James reminded them. "Maybe there's another building we're supposed to go to?" He unzipped his backpack, pulled out a folded-up tourist map of the entire island, and held it out for all three to look at.

"Industries Building." Emily pointed to a rectangle down by the coastline. "That starts with *I*."

"But no *S*," Nisha pointed out. "It does end in an *S*, though."

"Maybe it's not a place that starts with *IS*. Maybe our answer is incomplete and we're still supposed to follow Anglin and Morris," James suggested. "Maybe we need to go where they went next."

"You mean crawl through the hole in that cell? Are we allowed to do that?" Emily asked.

"If we're allowed, I don't want to," Nisha said with a shudder. "Would we even fit through there?"

"If grown men did, we should be able to," Emily said.

"They were escaping prison," James added. "It's not like it was designed with comfort in mind."

The cell door was locked, however. "There must be a door that accesses the utility corridor," Nisha said.

"Oh!" James's eyes brightened. "There was a glass door at that end that shows the space in between the cellblocks. I noticed it when we talked to the guard, and I thought it was weird they made the door see-through."

"Let's go check it out," Emily said.

They ran to the end of the cellblock to see what they'd find. Just as James had said, a glass door sealed off the space between the rows of cells. The utility corridor was a narrow, dimly lit alley with boring things like pipes and ductwork. A combination lock told them they wouldn't be opening the door.

James pressed his nose to the glass and cupped his hands around his eyes. "Hey! There's something posted in there. Can you see? I think it's a sign." He stepped away to give someone else a chance.

Nisha peered through the glass and slowly read out loud, "'The first . . . is for a . . . boat'? 'On the sea'?" She stepped back. "It's hard to make out, but I think that's the first line."

After taking turns and double- and triple-checking to make sure they were all in agreement, Nisha wrote in her notebook:

The first is for a boat on the sea

The second is for the job of a key

The third is for what's keeping you dry

The fourth is for colors in the sky

These four combined will unlock

the pronoun that helps you off this rock

"It's a riddle!" Nisha said.

"A boat on the sea? That could be all sorts of things," Emily said. "Battleship. Sailboat. Yacht. Dinghy. Skiff."

"Look at the last one," Nisha said. "That has to be *rainbow*, don't you think? So the letter *R*?"

"Or sunset," James said. "And the job of a key is to lock or unlock something."

"A jacket keeps you dry, or an umbrella," Emily said.

Nisha jotted down a quick list of the possible letters they'd come up with for each position.

B S Y D
L U
J U
R S

"I can't think of any four-letter word that has a *J* as the third letter. And if the third letter is *U*, then the second letter wouldn't also be *U*," Emily said.

Nisha revised their list accordingly:

B S Y D
L Ʉ
Ɉ U
R S

"Blur!" James called out. "I can make the word *blur* out of those letters."

"Also *slur*," Emily added. "But neither of those words is a pronoun. A pronoun would be something like he, she, or you."

They studied the original riddle for a minute, and then Nisha suggested, "Maybe there's more that a key can do besides lock or unlock."

"Like the key to a cipher can solve," James said.

"And what about a piano key? Its job would be to make music," Emily added.

"But using *M* or *S* with the other letters doesn't create another word," Nisha said.

"Oh! What about *open*?" Emily asked. "If you unlock a door with a key, you can open it."

Nisha updated her list of letters, and a pathway appeared, hopping from one letter down to another to form a word that was also a pronoun:

B S Y D
L Ø O
Ж U
S R

"*Your!*" they said in unison.

Emily and her friends jumped up and down, excited to have found and solved the second of what they hoped were Errol Roy's puzzles, when a peppy voice asked, "What did we find, gang?"

CHAPTER 27

STANDING BEHIND them were Fiona and her mother. "So where's the puzzle?" Fiona asked. Her wide-open eyes and smile made it seem like a friendly question, but her mother's rigid stance and mouth pinched in concentration as she appeared to scan the area for puzzles said otherwise.

Emily realized that because the riddle had been hung inside the utility corridor, you'd only really notice it if you pressed your face up to the glass door.

"We won't spoil the fun by telling you," Emily said. She couldn't resist adding, "We're on our way to the third puzzle now."

Mrs. Duncan bristled. "You've found two of Mr. Roy's four already? How do you know they're part of his solution?"

Over his shoulder, James called to them, "You'll figure it out."

They found a quiet corner between Michigan Avenue and the plastic wall with the plywood door that closed off A-Block.

"The first two puzzles were in locations along the prisoners' escape route," James recounted. "After getting into the utility corridor, they climbed to the roof, slid down a pipe, climbed a barbed-wire fence, and entered the water near an old power plant."

Nisha shuddered. "I am *not* doing those things. Mr. Griswold is crazy if he expects us to."

"Maybe there's a normal way to get to the roof," Emily pondered. "Stairs or an elevator with roof access—"

Her words were cut off by ringing bells, the kind you hear on a game show when someone wins a prize. Hollister's voice echoed over the loudspeaker.

"Hey, folks! We have a group of detectives who think they've solved the case! Join us in the dining hall to see if their solution is correct!"

"Already?" Nisha said.

"It feels like we've only been playing for an hour." James's shoulders slumped in disappointment.

Funny how quickly they could go from feeling confident they were doing well to plummeting to the bottom. Contestants hurried from all corners of the prison to enter the dining hall, eager to learn if the mystery had been solved. Even park rangers and security tagged along.

James came to a sudden halt when they entered the

dining hall. "You've got to be kidding," he said when he saw who stood on the platform with Hollister and Errol Roy.

The team claiming to have won was Bookacuda and his cronies.

Ugh. Emily could already imagine the gloating that would surely ensue if Bookacuda's solution was correct. He'd stand exactly as he was now, with his skinny frame ramrod straight and his pale, freckled face tilted up, like he was trying to stretch himself a couple of inches taller than he actually was. He'd boast about how much more impressive his win was than cracking a historical cipher that had only gone unbroken for so long because people stopped paying attention to it, or solving the clues in a Book Scavenger game nobody else was even playing.

Hollister swooped an arm in a welcoming gesture, encouraging everyone to gather around. Errol Roy stood behind him, bundled in his coat with his arms folded over the front like he was freezing. The temperature inside the prison had crept down with the sun, so Emily couldn't blame him, but he looked miserable, like he'd eaten something that disagreed with him.

Maddie was in the gathering crowd, standing off to one side of the platform by herself. Emily was still upset with her for having been so quick to believe the accusations about her brother, but there was something about how she stood a few feet removed from anyone else, shoulders hunched forward, that made Emily soften. Emily had spent years being the outsider, the lonely girl, the one without a group of friends, and she didn't want anyone else to feel that way, even someone Emily was annoyed with.

Emily had wondered why Hollister had made the announcement and not Mr. Griswold, but as she scanned the dining hall, she saw that both Matthew and the publisher were missing from the audience.

They must still be talking. She wondered if their absence was a good or bad sign about their conversation. Maybe Mr. Griswold *didn't* believe Matthew. Maybe the fact that a stolen bracelet had been in her brother's pocket was enough to convince Mr. Griswold. Maybe Mr. Griswold was calling their parents and sending Matthew back alone on a ferry right that very minute.

Emily wished her brother was here.

Her memory replayed the look Matthew had given her when she'd hesitated to speak up on his behalf. He was her brother, and while Matthew could be impulsive or outspoken, he wouldn't steal. And he wasn't the sort who would do anything in order to win. He was competitive with himself, but what mattered to him the most was having fun while playing the game, not whether he came in first. That was why he'd been so much fun to play Book Scavenger with when they were younger. He'd come up with elaborate stories—they were spies on a mission or aliens who'd just landed on Earth—and the adventures they'd have on their way to find hidden books were often more fun than the actual book-finding part.

Instead of standing here, thinking all these things about her brother, Emily realized she should go tell them to Mr. Griswold. She might not have spoken up for Matthew earlier, but it wasn't too late. Even if he wasn't in trouble, she wanted him to know she supported him.

"I'll be right back," she whispered to James and Nisha.

"You okay?" James asked.

"I'm going to check on Matthew," she said.

James nodded. Emily inched her way through the crowd. When she reached the outer fringe, she spotted Lucy Leonard on the outskirts of the room. While everyone else was coming *into* the dining hall and all eyes were on the stage, the author slipped out to the cellblocks.

Emily followed. She told herself this was likely the way to Mr. Griswold and Matthew—she assumed they were somewhere in the administrative area, which was across the cellblocks from the dining hall—but she was also curious about what Lucy Leonard could be up to. Every time Emily had observed her this evening, she'd been slightly odd. Not really socializing with anyone, although Emily did remember her joining in the group of people who'd helped look for Fiona's bracelet.

In fact . . .

Emily slowed her walking as something occurred to her.

Lucy Leonard had been on the ferry when Fiona lost her bracelet.

She'd also collided with Matthew before he'd been caught by Errol Roy. If planting the bracelet in her brother's pocket had been premeditated, that would have given her a good opportunity. And she'd seemed distracted when Emily had asked her about Book Scavenger and had hurried away.

What if Lucy Leonard had found the bracelet on the ferry, and then later dropped it in Matthew's pocket when he was too distracted to notice?

Why Lucy Leonard would do this, Emily had no idea. But the more she thought about it, the more it seemed like the only feasible explanation for Matthew's situation.

Her brother had been framed.

CHAPTER 28

EMILY SNUCK OUT of the dining hall into the cell-block area just in time to see Lucy turn onto Michigan Avenue. When Emily turned the corner, the corridor was empty and lit only by the solitary bulbs that hung in each cell up all three tiers. The skylights high above had deepened into a dark blue. Peering down the shadowy hallway that led to the cordoned-off A-Block, Emily noticed that the plywood door had been left ever so slightly ajar.

Were her eyes playing tricks on her? Emily stepped closer. The latch had been rotated to hang down on the sheet of wood. Looking behind her once more, Emily inched the plywood open and squeezed through to the other side.

She found herself in a concrete room, three stories tall like the rest of the prison. The long wall had windows that spanned the second and third floors, but they were blocked on the outside by more scaffolding wrapped in white plastic sheeting. Having windows but not being able to see outside made the room claustrophobic. The room served as an entry space to the A-Block cells, which were cordoned off by a cage wall that spanned all three stories. There was a gate in the cage wall that had been left wide open.

A voice inside Emily questioned what exactly she was doing, why she was walking back here where she knew full well she shouldn't be. She should turn around, and forget Lucy Leonard, and find her brother and apologize, and return to her friends, and offer fake congratulations to Bookacuda, and grin and bear it while he rubbed in his win.

But if her brother had been set up, she wanted to clear his name, and she wanted to understand why.

Emily walked through the open gate into A-Block, her heart beating rapidly.

The faint glow of moon cast enough light for her to make out the vertical silver slats of the jail-cell doors to her right, and the banisters overhead for the walkways on the second and third tiers. The insides of the cells were black, the kind of black that would have her imagining lurking men or creatures if she stared long enough, so she faced straight ahead to the long corridor.

Emily's sneakers squeaked softly on the concrete floor as she walked to the other end. It was incredibly quiet over here. When she'd first walked through the makeshift plywood door she'd been able to hear the distant reverberations of Hollister's voice, but not anymore.

Lucy Leonard was nowhere to be seen.

The shadow of something solid and square loomed ahead of her, like a very large box, but when Emily got close enough, she could see that it wasn't a box, but waist-high walls that enclosed a staircase leading underground.

The dungeon.

Emily stood at the top of the stairs staring down, wondering if that was where Lucy had gone. There was no other option, unless Emily had been mistaken about her entering the plywood door in the first place.

The stairs were steep and ended in darkness. In the faint light, Emily could see strips of paint peeled away from stairwell walls.

Emily was starting to doubt the task that she'd given herself when a loud metallic clang made her jump. Her heart nearly shot through her nose. Though the cellblock was dimly lit, she could see well enough to make out that the cage wall no longer had an open rectangle of space—someone had shut the cage door behind her.

Emily ran back to the gate and pushed on it. Locked.

"Hello?" Emily called. "Hello?"

Silence.

How had this happened? Had a park ranger come in and closed it, without first checking to see if anyone was in this area? She pressed her cheek to the wires, straining for a better look at the area she'd first entered into after stepping beyond the plywood door. Her stomach tightened when she saw the shadow of a person walking away.

"Hey, I'm in here!"

The shadow was tall and willowy, with a halo of tight curls springing from its head.

"Fiona?" Emily called.

But Fiona, if that was who it was, kept moving until Emily couldn't see her anymore. Emily hooked her fingers through the grid of wires and pushed and pulled and pushed and pulled. The door clanged, but it didn't open.

She waited a beat longer before calling one more time. "Hello?"

More silence.

Emily was trapped in Alcatraz A-Block, and the only person who knew where she was had probably been the one to lock her in.

CHAPTER 29

ERROL ROY needed to get off this island. The musty concrete smell mixed with the rich foods being served was making him feel ill. Alcatraz had an energy of its own, and he could sense it infecting him, twisting his mind into knots. Every passing minute, as Hollister waved contestants into the dining hall and waited for people to gather, was excruciating.

Finally the bookseller had a trio of kids on the stage.

"What is the answer you've come up with?" Hollister asked, extending the microphone to the young contestants.

Errol Roy pulled his handkerchief from his pocket and pressed it to his temple.

Instead of leaning over to speak into the mic, the short boy with a sharp nose and beady eyes grabbed it from the bookseller's hands. With the cockiness of a kid at a spelling bee who knew he was reciting the winning word, he said, "Anglin and Morris. That's the answer."

Roy straightened.

The audience was mostly silent, other than a few hushed exchanges here and there.

Hollister turned to Roy, an eager smile on his face. "Did they get it right?"

"No," Roy said.

He'd been so braced to hear the correct answer that he couldn't quite believe it himself. He simultaneously wanted this day to be over and didn't, and now that he knew the game would continue, he wasn't sure whether he should feel relief or anguish.

The audience erupted in excited cheers that were cut off when the same young boy who'd guessed the wrong answer stomped his foot and shouted at Roy, "It is *too* correct!"

Roy's eyebrows shot up; he was surprised and a little amused.

"It has to be the answer!" The boy—Errol had heard him referred to as Bookacuda—continued. "The Goldfish clue said one sixty-five, which we figured out was the cell number where that guy was reading a book and—"

Mr. Griswold's assistant, Jack, spoke up from the audience. "I'm sorry, did you say 'Goldfish clue'?"

"Yes!" Bookacuda threw up his hands like he'd been explaining rain is wet. "The one with the crackers."

Jack looked confused. "There wasn't any Goldfish clue."

The boy pressed his mouth into a thin, mean line. "Yes, there was." He nudged the boy who stood behind him. "Show them."

The older-looking boy unzipped his backpack and it fell open. Orange, fish-shaped crackers poured onto the floor, along with squares of paper that fluttered down.

"See?!" Bookacuda waved to the snack food with an impatient hand, but Hollister was frowning.

"You thought that was a puzzle for the game, and you removed it?" he asked. "Sabotaging is against the rules, whether the puzzle is fake or real."

The kid's beady eyes widened. Roy tuned out the rest of their exchange, fixating on the squares of paper that had fallen from the boy's backpack. One had landed near Errol's shoe. It was the letter D cut from a magazine. Nearby was an S and an E.

His breath felt trapped, like he'd been dunked underwater. His hand found its way to his pocket, and with shaky fingers he removed the crumpled note he'd found when he fell off the tram.

"Why did you do this?" Errol thrust the paper under Bookacuda's nose. The boy's pale face became even paler.

"That wasn't meant for you. . . . I . . ." he stammered.

"Liar!" Errol roared. The note shook in his hand,

and he imagined his face was crimson. Hollister placed a calming hand on his shoulder.

A boy standing near the stage piped up. "Hey—I think that was meant for me and Emily!"

"For you, James?" Hollister asked. He looked around the dining hall. "Where *is* Emily?"

"She's with Mr. Griswold and Matthew," James replied. "She and I both got notes like that at school, and then there was another one in her backpack when we got on the ferry. We didn't know who sent them, but apparently"—he pointed an accusing finger at Bookacuda—"he was trying to scare us out of the game."

The idea that the note hadn't been meant for him did nothing to calm Errol. The damage had been done. The words he'd read on the paper had him second-guessing everything on this blasted island from the moment he'd stepped off the tram.

"Then explain how it ended up with me!" Errol boomed.

Bookacuda had crossed his arms, attempting to appear tough, but he shrank back. "I . . . I don't know, sir," he said meekly.

The boy and girl standing on the platform behind their apparent ringleader exchanged a look.

"James is right," the tall boy said quickly. "Bookacuda did want to scare them out of the game."

"He said it would be funny," the girl added.

Bookacuda flinched as if he'd been punched. He

spun to face his supposed friends. "Traitors," he growled, his hands in fists at his sides.

"How did you get the notes into our lockers?" James asked. "Aren't you from Nebraska?"

"*He* is." The girl jerked a thumb in Bookacuda's direction. "We're all friends from online, through Book Scavenger. I go to school in the East Bay."

"I go to Booker, with you," the tall boy said to James. "I found where your lockers are and dropped the notes in them. It was Bookacuda's idea, but I was the one who did it. I'm sorry if they scared you guys."

Bookacuda shoved his friend. "Stop blabbing! What's wrong with you?"

"Hey, hey." Jack jumped onto the platform from the audience and stepped between the two boys.

Hollister shook his head and scolded Bookacuda. "These notes are enough to disqualify you from the game, not to mention purposely sabotaging something you thought was a puzzle—don't get yourself in even more trouble by starting a fight."

The tall boy was undeterred by Bookacuda's anger, and he turned to Errol Roy. "We didn't mean for you to get that note. Honest. We left it when we took Emily's backpack to hide on the dock. She was supposed to find the note, not you. I'm sorry about that, too."

The anger drained from Errol, making him feel very tired. "I need to go sit," he said to Hollister, or maybe he only thought it in his head. Regardless, Hollister was too wrapped up in resolving the drama to respond.

As Errol stepped down from the platform, a girl with short brown hair came forward. To Bookacuda she said, "Did you say you stole *Emily's* backpack? That wasn't her backpack, you dimwit, it was mine."

The audience had begun to dissipate as soon as players realized the game could still be won, but some had stayed either to listen to the argument or to solve puzzles in the room. Errol Roy shuffled among the people remaining in the dining hall, avoiding eye contact, and headed toward the cell house. The shrill voices carried on behind him, but he tuned everything out.

All he wanted to do was get back to his belongings and get off this island.

CHAPTER 30

"OKAY," EMILY SAID to herself. She hooked her hands around her backpack straps and paced back and forth. "Okay."

What did she have in her backpack that could help her? Matthew had his lock-picking kit—that sure would be useful right about now, although because of the chicken-wire nature of the cage, she wouldn't be able to reach through to the locked handle anyway. And he had the phone. All she'd brought was paper: her notebook and lists and books—fat lot of good that was going to do her. She wasn't even the one with a flashlight in her backpack, although she *had* packed her night-vision goggles. Those might come in handy, since she was pretty sure she'd have to brave the dungeon in order to find another way out.

The walk back to the stairwell felt longer this time, and the darkened cells seemed more shadowy, and their emptiness more questionable. Emily kept thinking something moved from the corner of her eye, but she was too afraid to look. It was her imagination, she told herself, or the moonlight filtering through the plastic-covered windows. And anyway, she reasoned further, if someone was actually in the shadows watching her, then they must not want to hurt her or they would have already tried to. It was like what they say about snakes—snakes only lash out if you take them by surprise.

Somehow that reasoning didn't ease her racing heart.

Emily stood at the top of the stairs that led down into a black void. Her choices were to wait in this room where the shadows felt like they had eyes and hope someone came looking for her, or to be proactive, brave the dungeon, and look for another way out.

Emily strapped the goggles onto her head, took a deep breath, and descended into the dungeon.

The stairs were steep and short. Anyone with big feet would have trouble walking down them, but Emily's sneakers fit the width perfectly. Her night-vision goggles washed everything in a dim green light. When she reached the bottom, she could make out the outlines of bricks on the floors and walls. She shuffled forward, hyperaware of how loud her breathing sounded, and followed a zigzagging corridor that led to a space that seemed to be a cross between a room and a very wide hallway.

It smelled like a cave down here. To her right were arched openings. It was getting harder for her to see— she'd forgotten that the goggles worked best outside, with moonlight—but through the arched openings there appeared to be tiny rooms, like the jail cells upstairs, but there were no bars or doors. Up ahead it looked like the path either hit a wall or turned a corner. Emily swallowed and the sound seemed so loud, like a boulder plunked into a pool.

What was she doing, searching for a way out of a dungeon she knew nothing about? Her skin felt chilled and exposed under her ponytail, and her neck hairs were on high alert. But going back upstairs to stand at the cage door and yell until somebody heard her didn't seem like a better option. Surely Fiona would alert people— eventually—that she was back here? *Someone* would find her. Wouldn't they?

Emily concentrated on breathing steadily and staying calm, but it was a losing battle. The hopelessness of her situation and the dark and being afraid were making her chest tighten. It was getting harder to breathe steadily and evenly.

A distant but furious roar made Emily go completely numb, and then her heart started pounding rapidly.

What in the world *was* that? Was that a person? Could that be an animal? She had no clue what might be kept in the dungeons of Alcatraz, but she was suddenly remembering the Greek myth about the Minotaur who lived in a labyrinth.

Emily didn't know what to do. Before she could make a decision and act, light bounced on the wall up ahead, and then rounded the corner, beaming from the top of Lucy Leonard's head. A bloodcurdling scream ricocheted around the cavernous room.

Emily squeezed her eyes shut. She wasn't sure if she or Lucy was screaming. Perhaps it was both of them.

"What are you doing here?!" Lucy Leonard finally yelled. "What is on your head?"

Emily's hands flew up to her face. Her heart was doing a frantic dance in her chest. "What is on *your* head?" she shot back.

"It's a headlamp," Lucy replied, her voice less shouty.

"I'm wearing night-vision goggles." Emily's words came out quickly. She took a deep breath. "They don't work so well in here," she added.

"Why in the world are you down here?" Lucy asked her. "You should be out there playing the game."

"So should you!" Emily argued back. "And you *shouldn't* be framing my brother."

"Framing your . . . what?"

"My brother! You stuck that bracelet in his pocket."

"I . . . what?" Lucy Leonard let out a long sigh. "Look, I have no idea what you're talking about."

Emily was thankful for the pressure of her goggles against her eyes, because her nose stung and tears were threatening to fall. Everything was getting to her—the darkness and the musky smell of being underground, her brother being called a thief, Fiona trapping her in A-Block.

Emily pressed her back against the wall and slid to a sitting position on the floor. The bricks were so cold, it felt like ice chilling her jeans. Tears slid from her eyes and she pushed the night-vision goggles onto her forehead so she could rub them away.

"Hey," Lucy said. She crouched next to her. "Hey, it's okay. I don't understand what's going on with your brother, but I'm sure things will work out. Come on, let's get out of here. I'm giving up on my mission anyway, so I'll head back with you, and maybe I can help you sort things out."

"We can't," Emily moaned. "We're trapped."

Lucy tugged on her arm. "Now you're being dramatic. We're not trapped."

"Yes, we are," Emily said. "Fiona closed the gate to A-Block behind me, and it's locked."

"It's . . . what?!" Lucy's headlamp whizzed to the right and left, like she was frantically trying to get her bearings. "Are you serious? Why didn't you lead with that?"

Lucy hurried out of the dungeon the way they'd come in, with Emily following behind. The woman ran to the closed gate and tested it for herself. They both rattled the cage door as loudly as they could, but again nobody came.

Lucy pulled a cell phone from her knapsack, pressing a button so the screen lit up. "No service, of course." She sighed. "Okay, let's think. Let's think." She started pacing and tapping her phone into the palm of her hand. "If we can't get out this way, we can go back into the dungeon and use the tunnels. If we can find our way to the morgue, there might be an entry point into it from the tunnel."

"The *morgue*? Like where they keep the dead people?" Emily shivered.

"Mm-hmm." Lucy nodded absentmindedly, mulling over her proposed plan. She explained, "The morgue was built on top of an entrance to an old military tunnel from the 1870s."

Finally Lucy registered Emily's alarm. "It hasn't been used in decades," she reassured her. "And even when the prison was active, it was barely used. They never performed autopsies on Alcatraz and most bodies were sent to the mainland." Lucy said all of that as if it would be reassuring.

It wasn't.

Lucy turned her back on the jail cells in A-Block and sliced her hand like she was cutting cake. "If this is east, and if this is south"—she rotated a quarter of a circle—"then the morgue would be . . ." She bobbed her head around, and Emily imagined she was visualizing a map. "Okay, I think I've got it."

Lucy led them back down the steep, shallow staircase into the dungeon. Her headlamp bounced off the brick walls, and Emily hurried to stay close. Her night-vision goggles were still up on her forehead, and she fidgeted with their strap as if it were a headband.

"What was your mission?" Emily asked as they walked.

"My what?"

"You said before you were down here on a mission," Emily reminded her.

Lucy shook her head, making the headlamp swoop across the dark expanse in front of them.

"My mission is *I'm an idiot*."

They turned a corner, then another, and Lucy slowed down, the light on her head illuminating every direction she looked. She stopped in front of an opening that looked more like a jagged hole punched through the brick than an official entry point. Vertical metal beams on either side appeared to hold up the tunnel roof.

"That's where we need to go."

"In there? Are we allowed?" Emily asked.

"Uh, kid, none of this is allowed." Lucy swung her arms wide. "You shouldn't have followed me back to

A-Block, and neither of us should be down here. As long as we don't move anything or dig or upset any of these metal support beams they've put in, we should be fine."

Should be rang in Emily's ears.

"How do you know all this? Where to go down here?" Emily asked. It occurred to her that maybe it was crazy for her to trust this adult she barely knew to lead her through the belly of Alcatraz.

"I've been studying the tunnels for a book I'm writing," Lucy said. "I'm fairly certain the opening to the morgue is right through there."

Well, Emily didn't feel like she had many options. And the sooner they got into this morgue, the sooner they would get out and back to her friends and brother. Emily straightened her shoulders and steeled her resolve. Lucy climbed through first; then Emily took a deep breath and swung one leg over the bottom wall of the hole and climbed in after. She could reach her hands out on either side and feel cool brick walls. This area had much lower ceilings. They only had to go a few feet before Lucy stopped and looked up, her headlamp illuminating a recessed opening above them that was about as big as a medium-sized dog. Lucy reached through the opening and knocked on what sounded like wood.

"There it is. That's the hatch into the morgue."

CHAPTER 31

LUCY PUSHED AGAINST the door, testing it out. "This tunnel we're in used to not be accessible at all, but they've been working on restoring them. I don't think this is a very permanent door, so I was hoping . . ." She pushed against it again, straining.

Emily stood on her tiptoes and pushed with her. They knocked and pounded and pressed until finally the wood gave way and fell with a clatter on the other side of the opening.

Emily and Lucy stared up into the black chasm.

"I'll give you a boost, and you climb through first," Lucy said. "I'll follow right behind."

"You want me to go first? Into a morgue?!"

"I don't think we have a choice. I can climb through first, but then how would you get up?"

Lucy had a point.

Emily closed her eyes, planning to visualize being

in her bedroom instead of inside a morgue at night on Alcatraz.

"Okay," Emily said, her eyes still shut.

But then she heard James's voice, far-off but distinct, call out, "See, there's the water tower!"

Emily's eyes popped open. "My friends!" she said.

"Those voices?" Lucy asked.

"Yes, that was James."

"Do you think they're looking for you?"

"It sounds like they're looking for a . . . water tower? I thought the game was over."

"Hello!" Lucy hollered. Emily joined in, too. They tossed their heads back and yelled at the top of their lungs, which felt oddly freeing. For a second Emily could forget she was trapped underground on Alcatraz.

Their shouts faded, and they listened, but Emily couldn't hear her friends anymore.

"If they're hunting for a clue near the water tower," Lucy said, "then they'll likely be coming back this way. If we can get ourselves up there, we'll have a better chance at catching their attention."

This time Emily didn't hesitate when Lucy laced her fingers together and offered her hands as a step for Emily's foot.

The next thing she knew, she was launched into the dark void. Her forearms folded over the cold, hard lip of the hole; then she pulled herself forward, her backpack scraping the edge of the opening, and crawled out the hole onto the floor.

She was in the very back of the morgue and could see now that the hatch was like a hobbit-sized door in the floor. Crouching in the dark, Emily completely forgot her plan to keep her eyes closed.

The morgue was a small space, maybe the size of a couple of jail cells, and mostly empty other than an old bench and an ancient piece of industrial equipment Emily was currently wedged next to. The back part of the morgue, where she and the bulbous machine were, was in an alcove, and when she straightened, she had to be mindful of both the low ceiling and the pipes that ran from the contraption. When she stepped out of the alcove into the small main area, the ceiling was much higher and made of windows, like a greenhouse roof, but the glass was opaque from age and dirt and the shadows of overgrown vines.

Once Lucy was out of the tunnel and in the morgue next to her, they stepped to the front of the space and tried to twist the handle of the main door, but it was locked from the outside. The windows that weren't overgrown with ivy had been rusted shut.

"Are we trapped in here?" Emily asked. She attempted to swallow the panic rising up her throat. When she was stuck in A-Block, at least Fiona knew she was there, but nobody would think to check the morgue.

"I wouldn't say trapped. We can also go back through the dungeon to where we started."

Emily didn't know which place would be worse to wait in, and the thought of climbing back into the dark

and clammy tunnels under Alcatraz made her shiver.

"Remember, your friends passed by," Lucy reminded her. "Let's stay put and see if we can get their attention on their way back."

"Okay." Emily nodded curtly, her ponytail bobbing against her neck.

Lucy checked her phone again. "Yes! I've got bars. Of course my battery's nearly dead."

"Can you text my brother?" Emily asked. "He has his phone with him."

Lucy handed over the phone, and Emily typed in her messages:

This is Emily.
I'm trapped in the morgue.
And I'm sorry I didn't have your back.

"Now I guess we wait," Lucy said. She pulled off her headlamp and roughed up her hair where the straps had been.

They perched on the edge of a bench that had moss growing over it. The morgue smelled like salt water and fog, and sitting there in the darkness, Emily was reminded of Nisha's fears of an Alcatraz ghost. Chills spread down her back as she imagined one in the alcove behind them, watching them. Emily wanted to think about anything else, so she asked Lucy, "Why did you say your mission was being an idiot?"

"Oh." Lucy snorted sheepishly. "It would bore you. It had to do with my next book."

"The one about Harriet Beecher Stowe?"

Lucy Leonard cocked her head to the side. "Good memory," she said. "It might surprise you to know I'm not here to play Mr. Griswold's game."

"Noooo," Emily said in mock outrage.

Lucy guffawed. "You guessed, huh? Well, my most recent book, *The Twain Conspiracy*, was pretty successful."

That seemed like an understatement, Emily thought, but she mm-hmmed to show she was listening.

"I'm under a lot of pressure to follow it up with something similar, specifically a true story about a historical figure of significance that reveals something previously unknown. And I'm an idiot because I came here on a fool's errand. I thought I'd be able to solve a one-hundred-and-fifty-year-old mystery."

Lucy nudged Emily with her elbow. "I suppose I'm talking to the wrong person for sympathy since you actually *did* solve a mystery that old."

Emily ducked her head and smiled. "What's the unsolved mystery you wanted to solve?" she asked.

"What happened to Frederick Stowe," Lucy replied.

"Frederick Stowe?"

Lucy nodded.

"Harriet Beecher Stowe's son disappeared in 1871 after arriving in San Francisco. He wrote his mother about plans to go out to sea and work on a ship, and that was the last she or anyone ever heard from him. There have been different theories about what might have happened. San Francisco was a rough town back then and there was a practice called *shanghaiing*, where people were kidnapped and made to work as indentured servants on ships. That's one possibility. Frederick struggled with alcohol addiction, so others propose he succumbed once again to addiction and didn't make a recovery. Others speculate that he purposely cut off his connection with his family because he suffered under the limelight of his mother's fame."

"Her books were popular?" Emily asked.

"Oh, her writing went beyond popular," Lucy replied. "It's been said that Abraham Lincoln once greeted Harriet Beecher Stowe with the words, 'So you're the little woman who wrote the book that started this great war,' referring to the Civil War. *Uncle Tom's Cabin* was popular *and* it spurred contentious political debate and fueled the fires of the Civil War."

Emily swung her legs on the bench as she considered this. "So what do you think happened to him?"

"I think he came to Alcatraz."

"Here?!" Emily said.

Lucy nodded. "In 1871, when Frederick Stowe arrived in San Francisco, this was Fort Alcatraz—the island was owned by the military. There was a citadel that was torn down in the 1900s, but the dungeon we were in, those rooms were part of it."

"Why do you think he came here?"

"*That*"—Lucy held up a finger—"is where my great discovery comes in. I found a letter."

"A letter?"

"Yes. A letter signed by a Frederick that was mixed in with Mark Twain's papers, of all places. I found it when I was researching *The Twain Conspiracy*. He and Harriet Beecher Stowe were neighbors for a period of time, toward the end of her life. My theory is the letter was misdelivered and Harriet never received it."

"That's so sad," Emily said. Being apart from her parents right that very moment, she imagined if she and Lucy remained trapped on Alcatraz and were never found, and her parents never learned what happened to her. Sitting in the tiny morgue illuminated only by diluted moonlight, the idea of never seeing her parents again was kind of freaking her out. The walls felt like they were pushing the darkness even closer to her, and the night felt eerily quiet except for a distant and steady *shhhh* of the bay waves.

"Did the letter say he was here?" Emily asked in a hushed voice.

"No, but it did say he had re-enlisted in the army. I found that interesting, but I didn't immediately make a connection to Alcatraz. But then, not too long after I found the letter, I heard about an Alcatraz urban legend. Supposedly there is writing in the citadel and underground tunnels that dates back to the 1800s. Signatures of some of the men who were here, that sort of thing. But what rang some bells for me is that there is rumored to be a longer quote written on the walls down there that says something about not giving up, and soon the tide will turn.

"That resonated because there is a fairly well-known Harriet Beecher Stowe quote from a book she wrote a couple of years before Frederick disappeared called *Oldtown Folks*. It goes like this: 'When you get into a tight place, and everything goes against you till it seems as if you couldn't hold on a minute longer, never give up then, for that's just the place and time that the tide'll turn.'"

"But, I thought you said you *didn't* solve the mystery?" Emily said. "It sounds to me like you did."

"What I have is a theory. I don't have any proof other than the letter. And, even if I can get that verified as being from Frederick, it will only prove that he survived, but doesn't really explain what happened to him. Even if I located the quote, I'm not sure that would solve the mystery conclusively, either, although it would certainly strengthen my case." Lucy sighed. "It was a harebrained idea, anyway."

A distant foghorn gave a mournful moan, as if it was as discouraged as Lucy about her Stowe book.

"You don't have to give up on the book, though," Emily said. "Why don't you come back to Alcatraz another day? Ask one of the park rangers to show you around the dungeon."

"That's just it—I did ask, but they won't grant access to the tunnels right now because of all the reconstruction projects they're doing. And I don't have time to wait because of my deadlines. When I heard about Mr. Griswold's game, I was enticed by the idea of coming to the island when there wouldn't be as many people, and I might possibly find my way into the tunnels. . . ."

Lucy waved her hands like *good riddance*. "It was a ridiculous idea born out of desperation. You're probably too young to understand any of this, but once you achieve a moment of success, there can be a lot of pressure to live up to expectations and regurgitate that success over and over. It's almost like a paranoia—you feel like all eyes are on you, even though the rational part of your brain knows all eyes aren't, and people probably don't care as much as you think. But then that can mess with you, too—the idea that people don't care at all."

That actually made complete sense to Emily.

"You think more about what other people are thinking and doing," Emily said slowly, "and then you act differently because of that, instead of doing something the way you normally would."

Lucy's shadow straightened. "Exactly! That's exactly it. After this whole experience, I wonder if I'm really cut out for this writer's life."

It surprised Emily that someone like Lucy Leonard—whom she'd seen sit on a stage talking to a theater full of people all riveted by what she had to say, and who could create a book that people like Emily's mom went nuts over—could doubt what she was doing.

"Don't you enjoy it? Being a writer?" Emily asked.

"I love it," Lucy replied. "It's challenging, but then again, the most rewarding things we do are often challenging." She was quiet a moment, then added, "I guess that's my answer, isn't it?"

CHAPTER 32

THE TWO SAT silently in the morgue waiting for someone to come. Emily scuffed her sneakers back and forth on the cement floor. Lucy checked her phone to see if Matthew had responded to the texts. But there was nothing.

Finally there was a distant noise that Emily might have mistaken for a birdcall if she hadn't known her friends had passed by earlier. "I think that's them! I think that's James!"

Emily and Lucy jumped up, ran to the door, and pounded on it, yelling and rattling the handle. Then they were quiet, listening to see if anyone approached. Nothing. They repeated the process. This time Emily could hear her friends' voices more distinctly, but it didn't sound like they were calling for her or coming nearer to the morgue.

"I have an idea," Emily said. "I need something hard that I can knock with."

Lucy slipped her headlamp back on and scanned the light across the debris in the morgue. Emily spotted a loose piece of pipe and used it to hammer on the door in the pattern she and James used when they traded messages in their bucket pulley.

Thud. Thud-thud-thud. Thud.

She paused for a few seconds, then repeated the pattern.

Thud. Thud-thud-thud. Thud.

After doing this over and over, Emily started to worry that it was all futile, that she'd never get out of this morgue and she'd be left here stranded on Alcatraz forever, when she heard a far-off voice call, "Emily?"

"Yes!" she said. She repeated the knocking pattern, and this time she and Lucy yelled at the top of their lungs, too, and Lucy rattled the door of the morgue.

"Emily?" James's voice was closer, and then it was right outside. "Are you in there?"

"Yes!" Emily shouted, so relieved she thought she might burst into tears. "I'm in here with Lucy Leonard!"

Emily was surprised to hear Maddie's voice ask, "Why in the world are you in the morgue? And who's Lucy Leonard?"

Nisha shrieked. "That's a morgue?! Are you stuck with dead bodies?! Is Lucy Leonard a ghost? I knew there were going to be ghosts!" she wailed.

"I'm not a ghost," Lucy called out, and Nisha shrieked again.

"Nisha, it's okay," Emily called. "There are no dead bodies."

Funny that she was the one locked in a morgue, but was calming other people down.

"She has the garlic in her hand," James announced.

"Well, we're one step closer to making spaghetti sauce, but that won't help us get out of here," Lucy said. "Can one of you go find Garrison Griswold? Or a park ranger?"

"I'll do that!" Nisha shouted. Emily was sure Nisha was eager to run as far away from a morgue as she could.

One of the windows rattled, making Emily jump and shout, "Eep!"

"Sorry." James's voice came through the glass. "I thought maybe this would open. Hey, maybe one of my scytales can work as a lever!"

There was a series of knocks at the window as Emily imagined James testing out the various cylindrical objects he had in his bag.

"Your friends keep garlic and scytales on hand?" Lucy asked.

Emily shrugged. "They like to be prepared."

Another voice outside the morgue said, "Dude, what are you doing, James? Are you trying to break in with a can of Cheez Whiz?"

"Matthew!" Emily shouted, pounding the palm of her hand against the door.

The handle of the door started jiggling, and Lucy stood up from the bench. "Is that a ranger? Griswold? Someone with a key?"

"No, they're not here yet. It's me," Matthew said. "I'm trying out my lock-picking kit."

"Lock-picking kit? Your friends really do travel prepared," Lucy said to Emily, before sitting back down.

"I thought you guys were together," James said, meaning Emily and her brother.

"I thought she was with you all," Matthew replied.

"It's a long story," Emily called through the door.

"We've got a lot to fill you in on, too," James said. "The main headline is that Bookacuda was disqualified."

"*Disqualified?*" Emily asked. "How? Why?"

"Fiona and her mom, too," Matthew added.

This was news to her friends, as they joined Emily in a chorus of "What?!"

There was a loud click and a creak and then the door swung open. Matthew held up a little tool in his hand. "Picked it!"

Emily ran out and threw her arms around her brother's neck. Lucy stepped out after her, dusting off the back of her pants. She raised a hand and said, "I'm Lucy Leonard. An author, not a ghost."

"Well, that clears everything up," Maddie replied sarcastically.

"So how did Bookacuda get disqualified?" Emily asked.

"Well, for starters, he was the one who stole my

bag," Maddie announced. "And I'm sorry about how I acted with all of that." She looked from Emily to Matthew, including them both in her apology. "I was really dumb."

"Thanks, Maddie," Emily said, "but it's okay. We probably should have been more concerned when you lost your bag in the first place."

Coming down the hill from the prison was Mr. Griswold, a park ranger, and Nisha. Lucy put a hand on Emily's shoulder. "I'm going to tell Mr. Griswold I'm responsible for us being in the morgue, and you shouldn't be held accountable for my actions."

"Why?" Emily asked.

"You only followed me because you were worried about your brother—you wouldn't have gone into an off-limits area otherwise. You should be able to finish Unlock the Rock with your friends."

"Well . . . thank you," Emily said.

Lucy started up the hill and called over her shoulder, "Good luck with the game, Emily!"

Emily called after her, "Good luck with your book!"

Nisha ran down the hill, passing Lucy Leonard as she stopped to confer with the grown-ups.

"You're out!" Nisha said when she reached Emily. "How did you do that?"

"It seems ghosts are pretty good at unlocking doors," Emily replied.

"Ahhh!" Nisha spun around and ran straight back the way she'd come. Emily and her friends laughed.

As their group walked up the hill to the prison under the light of lampposts, James and Maddie filled Emily in on how Bookacuda and his friends were responsible for the notes they'd received and were disqualified because of that, as well as destroying what they thought was a real puzzle.

"What about Fiona?" Emily asked.

"Fiona planted the bracelet on me," Matthew said.

"Fiona?! But it was *her* bracelet." Even though she'd guessed the wrong person in Lucy, Emily did feel a little vindicated that she was right about someone having tried to set up her brother.

"I figured it out when I was talking to Mr. Griswold. I knew *I* didn't take the bracelet. But it had to get in my pocket somehow. When I thought back through everything, I realized she could have faked losing her bracelet on the ferry. People searched everywhere for it except in her own pockets. And then, when all those people were in that small office with Errol Roy, she could have easily dropped it in my pocket. It was light enough that I wouldn't have felt it.

"So then Mr. Griswold brought in Fiona and her mother, and Fiona confessed. I guess she was under a lot of pressure from her mom to win the game. Her mom is a huge Errol Roy fan and aspiring writer. I think she was hoping if she impressed him enough, he might help her get a book published or something."

"Why frame you, though? How does that help her? That makes no sense," Emily said.

"Because she knows I'm the *brains* of this operation, of course," Matthew said teasingly.

"I should have realized," Emily deadpanned.

"It did disrupt our game, though," Maddie pointed out. "I'm sure that's what she was hoping for. Matthew would be disqualified; we'd get distracted and lose focus."

"We have one more update for you, Emily," James said.

Emily wasn't sure she could handle anything else.

"Maddie, Nisha, and I found and solved the third puzzle," James said.

Emily squealed. She couldn't help it. All that time in the tunnels, she'd assumed Bookacuda had won. She was bursting with excitement to have another chance and couldn't stop bouncing.

"When we catch up with Nisha, we'll fill you in on the latest puzzle."

Matthew checked his phone as they jogged. "Twenty minutes left to figure out the solution in time to win Hollister the bonus money."

"Twenty minutes?" Emily said. "That's not much time at all. Let's hurry!"

CHAPTER 33

THE FIVE OF THEM gathered around a table in the dining hall. Maddie presided over their meeting, referring to Nisha's notes.

"The puzzle solutions we've found so far, in order, spell out *IS YOUR MAN*." She tapped each word for emphasis.

"Mr. Roy said we needed to identify the prisoner who escaped in his story," James said. "It sounds like we're missing the most important word."

Emily scrutinized the three words. "It looks like we missed the first puzzle. If you insert a name in there for the solution, the most natural spot is the beginning of the sentence."

"Yeah," Matthew agreed. "You wouldn't say *Is your man Joe*, unless you were asking it as a question."

"Which means the puzzle we missed would be before the jail cell," James said.

"But that's where the escape began," Maddie pointed out. "The clock hint told us to follow Anglin and Morris, and the entire escape began in their jail cells."

Matthew tipped his chair back and looked around the dining hall. "Maybe it's a puzzle in this room," he said. "This is where the game started for us, and maybe it's where the men made plans for their escape, too."

Emily jumped up from her chair. "Roast beef!"

"Seriously?" Matthew asked. "You want to eat right now? We don't have time for that!"

Emily shook her head. "Not to eat. It's a puzzle. At least I think it is. Remember the prisoner who told us to try the roast beef?"

Matthew sat forward, dropping the legs of his chair back to the floor with a thud. "I bet you're right."

James smacked his hand to his forehead. "Miss Linden gave us that clue in the library, too. What are we waiting for? Let's get some roast beef!"

All five of them didn't need to go to the counter, but that's what they did. A woman wearing a chef's hat stood behind a metal countertop. Even the kitchen had prison bars, which slid open to form a window for serving.

"We'll have the roast beef," James announced.

"Good choice," she said. The woman slid over a metal tray with two pieces of bread and a piece of paper sticking out from the middle.

"Aww, there's no actual meat? I'm starving," Matthew said.

James pulled out the paper and slid over the plate. "You can eat the bread," he said.

They scooted down to the end of the counter and studied the puzzle:

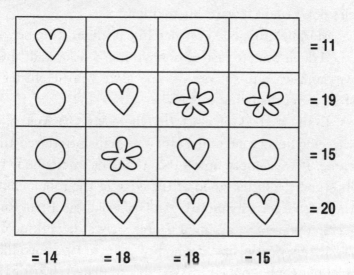

"Easy," Maddie announced.

She'd already written down five for the heart when Matthew yelped, "Stop!"

"Why?" James asked.

Maddie ignored him and solved the circle for two.

"Some puzzles are red herrings," Matthew said. "Before Errol Roy came in that office room and got mad at me, I saw the notes he'd read from lying on the desk, and I noticed there was a typo. *Some* was spelled *S-U-M*.

I thought that was weird, an author like him making a typo like that. But maybe it was a hint, and not a typo."

"I bet you're right!" James nodded. "The math puzzles don't count toward his solution."

Maddie dropped her pencil like it might sting her.

"I don't want to rush us or anything," Nisha said. "But we don't want to run out of time if we want Hollister's store to get the bonus money."

Emily studied the platform where Mr. Griswold had welcomed everyone and Errol Roy had introduced the game. It was empty now, other than the microphone in its stand. Hollister stood at the edge of the room, chatting with a security guard. Mr. Griswold and Errol Roy weren't present. A group of people were still working on the jigsaw puzzle, one of whom was Jack. It seemed like a lot of people stopped by the table to place a few pieces and then moved on to find another task in the game. A group of three was sitting at a table working out a problem on a piece of paper.

Emily looked back at the math sheet on the counter.

"Do you guys remember what the first clue was? The one Errol Roy read?"

"He said it wasn't right," James said.

Emily nodded. "He did, but didn't you tell me to pay close attention because he's well known for hiding details in plain sight?" She tapped the math worksheet again. "*Sum puzzles* was written into his opening statement.

He said it for all to hear; we're just conditioned to assume that that word, used in that context, would be *s-o-m-e* and not *s-u-m*. Maybe he did something similar with the first clue, and was only pretending it was wrong."

Everyone considered this idea and tried to remember what he'd read from the card.

"Was it *I know what you did*?" James asked.

"I think it had *secret* in it," Nisha said.

"*Everyone will find out your secret*?" Maddie said at the same time Emily guessed, "*What is your secret?*"

"Didn't Hollister pick up the card after Errol Roy dropped it on the floor?" James said.

"He's right there," Emily pointed out. "Let's ask him."

"Hey, kids!" Hollister greeted them as they ran up.

"Quick, Hollister," James said. "Do you still have that card? The one Errol Roy read in the beginning? We're close to winning you the money, but we need to hurry."

Hollister's eyebrows popped up. "Someone else asked to see that earlier. Roy said the card was wrong, didn't he?" As the bookseller spoke, he reached into his pocket and dug out the card.

James plucked it from his fingers. "Thanks, Hollister!"

They ran and sat on the edge of the platform, everyone crowding close to see. James read the card aloud:

I KNOW YOUR SECRET

"Some of the letters are different," Maddie pointed out.

"The *O*, *Y*, and *R*," Nisha added.

"Which spells Roy," Emily said.

"Roy? As in Errol Roy?" James asked.

"Did we just solve the game?" Nisha said, entirely uncertain.

Mr. Griswold entered the room and called out, "Attention, everyone! We have another team who thinks they might have cracked the case!"

Matthew's eyes widened. "How did he know that?"

"Are we sure we did, though?" James asked. "The solution doesn't make sense."

"Mr. Griswold didn't mean us," Emily said.

Mr. Quisling and Miss Linden entered behind Mr. Griswold and all three approached the platform. Mr. Quisling gave Emily and her friends a stiff smile. He looked somber, like he was on his way to do something he really didn't want to do. Miss Linden wiggled her fingers to them in a wave and did an excited shimmy with her shoulders. Mr. Griswold patted Steve affectionately as he stepped onto the platform behind them and crossed to the microphone.

"Greetings, contestants!" His voice rang throughout the room. "Please come to the dining hall to hear our latest theory from a team of detectives. And where's Errol Roy? Can you come to the stage to let them know if they've got it right, Mr. Roy?"

Contestants filed into the dining hall and gathered around the platform.

"Errol Roy?" Mr. Griswold said into the microphone once again. He caught Hollister's eye across the room and said, "You want to check the office? Maybe he can't hear me back there."

Hollister nodded and left the room. Mr. Griswold drummed his fingers on the microphone stand and said in a low, drawn-out voice, "Exciiiiting! Why don't you tell us your solution so we can all wait in suspense together to find out if you're right."

Mr. Quisling leaned to the microphone and said slowly and solemnly, "The solution we came up with is *Roy is your man.*"

Mr. Griswold tilted his head, perplexed. "That's a curious solution," he said.

Emily and her friends exchanged looks with one another, as the confused buzzing of conversations circulated the room. Hearing Mr. Quisling say it confirmed for Emily that they must be right, but what did it mean?

Hollister came back alone, a frown on his face.

"Where is he?" Mr. Griswold called over. His bright smile began to falter as he waited for the answer.

"He's gone," Hollister said.

CHAPTER 34

HOLLISTER HANDED Mr. Griswold an envelope. "I found this on the desk," he said.

Mr. Griswold slid a finger through the flap and unfolded a piece of paper, which he proceeded to read aloud:

> *Dear Readers,*
>
> *You know me as a fiction writer. It's what I do best. I never imagined I'd make money from telling lies—*
>
> *That's not true.*
>
> *I imagined it, but not in a way where so many people would support and encourage me, and would enjoy my lies. I am forever grateful for having had that opportunity, and that you accepted my stories so warmly.*
>
> *There is one more lie I must confess to now.*

You know me as Errol Roy, but I was born Clarence Anglin. As Clarence Anglin, I was inmate #1485 at Alcatraz. In 1962, I carried out an elaborate escape along with my brother John and Frank Morris. Some say the plan was a success because we were never heard from again.

I don't.

My brother and Frank didn't make it to land. Somehow I did, physically, but I have often felt Clarence Anglin died that night, too.

Luck saved me as I crossed the bay, but it was reading books that gave me a second chance at life. I made my way to Brazil where I found solace in Dashiell Hammett, a mystery writer I discovered while at Alcatraz. His personal story spoke to me us much as his writing. Dashiell Hammett began writing when he was bedridden with tuberculosis. Although I wasn't ill, I related to the extreme isolation. I admired what he was able to do with a story.

In 1976, the same year my third story was published, I moved back to the United States as Errol Roy. The rest of my story is well known. Some of you might be able to recount it better than I can myself.

I have to state, once again, that I acted alone today. Neither Garrison Griswold, nor the caretakers of Alcatraz, nor anyone involved with Unlock the Rock has known anything about my plans or my true identity.

It's a miracle I've made it this long, given the life I've led, and I don't know how much more time will be allotted to me. I would regret going into this dark night without revealing my truth, but I also can't face prison at my advanced age, which is surely where my story would end if I did not disappear once again.

My lawyer, who has no prior knowledge about my plans or my past identity, will be receiving instructions tomorrow to distribute a check to Hollister's bookstore in the amount of $100,000. (I have faith that Garrison Griswold's event will attract readers who can solve my puzzle within the time limit.) The rest of my wealth will be donated to the American Library Association to be distributed to community outreach programs that bring literacy and reading initiatives to prisons and juvenile-delinquent centers.

I know this is the coward's way out, to run away once more and not turn myself in with this confession. I apologize to any of my loyal readers who feel I've let them down. I hope you will appreciate my effort to come clean before my time is up, and leave you with one last story to remember.

—Errol Roy

CHAPTER 35

ERROL ROY sailed under a night sky masked with clouds. Behind him, Alcatraz was a shadowy mass. The dim lights of the cell house glowed like the embers of a fading fire.

It hadn't quite sunk in that he'd made it off the Rock for the second time. This escape was more luxurious compared to his last. Instead of a makeshift raft crafted from prison-issued raincoats, he'd paddled his kayak from Alcatraz to the marina where he kept his beloved *Effie Perine*, the catamaran he hoped would get him to Mexico and beyond. On his outing the night before, he'd used his dinghy to hide the kayak in the brush near one of the few accessible points on the Alcatraz coastline. Errol Roy had escaped once before, and he hoped he wouldn't get found this time, either, but he would take his chances.

Just as he always had.

Beyond the white light of *Effie*'s mast, the clouds shifted in the dark sky. Moonlight broke through and illuminated a pathway forward. Errol pointed the boat toward the yellow lights of the Golden Gate Bridge and the open sea beyond.

As he glided into his next uncertain chapter, he imagined the boat disappearing over the horizon, rings spreading behind like a peacock fanning its tail.

Errol Roy had escaped Alcatraz. Again.

CHAPTER

36

O N THE SUNDAY after Unlock the Rock, Emily and James pushed open the door to Hollister's, and the old familiar bells jangled, announcing their entrance. Emily had never thought she'd miss the sound of sleigh bells as much as she had.

"Hollister!" they called to the bookseller, and ran forward to give him a hug. Their families filed in the store behind them. They'd arrived early to help set up the grand reopening, but Mr. Griswold and Jack were already there, and Mr. Quisling and Miss Linden, too.

"Where would you like us to put this?" James's mom asked, holding up a stack of bamboo steamers. His mom and grandmother's catering business had offered to provide a dim sum bar for the event.

Hollister led them over to a long folding table, which Mr. Quisling and Jack were covering with a paper tablecloth.

"It looks like a brand-new store in here!" Emily marveled, turning in a circle to take it all in.

There were, of course, bookcases everywhere, filled with books, but Hollister had brightened the store considerably by painting them, and there was a new reclaimed-wood floor. The old spiral staircase in the back had been redone completely with wood risers that had the fronts painted to look like different book spines. The upstairs loft used to be a cluttered mass of boxes, but now it looked like it might be a reading nook—Emily made a note to check it out later.

There were endless touches of book art and whimsy—book-page lanterns dangled from the ceiling, and on the wall behind the register hung three books, each with its pages folded in a way that made it look like a word was jumping out.

Emily imagined she and James would spend many future afternoons after school exploring the new and improved store.

The bells on the door jingled and a woman's voice asked, "Am I in the right place for the party?"

Emily turned to see Lucy Leonard stepping inside the store.

"Ms. Leonard! Welcome!" Hollister hurried over to usher her inside.

"Oh, please, Hollister, call me Lucy," she said.

Emily's mom stared with her mouth open. "That isn't . . . is that . . . ?" She looked to Emily's dad, who was also analyzing Lucy curiously. Lucy gave them a polite smile as she passed by and tapped Emily on the shoulder with a "Hey there!"

Emily gave Lucy a hug and laughed at her mom's flabbergasted reaction.

"Mom, would you like to meet my new friend, Lucy?" she said.

"Your . . . *friend*? But how . . . last Monday you were, I mean, and now you're on a first-name basis?"

Emily had decided to keep Lucy Leonard a surprise for her mom, and it was as entertaining as she'd hoped it would be.

Lucy extended a hand. "Emily and I met at Unlock the Rock. She told me you enjoyed my book."

"Enjoyed it? *Enjoyed* it?" And Emily's mom was off and running, talking nonstop about how much *The Twain Conspiracy* meant to her, with Emily's dad chiming in every so often to say things like, "That's true! One day she was reading your book on the bus and missed so many stops, she was practically to Noe Valley before she realized!"

Emily was a little embarrassed at how gushy her parents were and wasn't sure if she should intervene, but Lucy glanced over and gave her a wink, so she figured it was all good.

Mr. Quisling came to stand next to James and said, "How are you hanging in there about Errol Roy?"

James threw his hands out and his head back, pantomiming being frozen in a state of disbelief.

Mr. Quisling nodded. "Yep, I'm still in shock myself, too."

"I can't believe there's been no sign of him," Miss Linden said.

"Four days." Mr. Quisling shook his head. "He clearly planned ahead for this, but the authorities might well catch up with him eventually."

Miss Linden rested a hand on James's shoulder. "You okay? He was a favorite of yours, wasn't he?"

"Yeah." James threaded his fingers through Steve, making him extra spiky. "I'm not sure what to think about it, to be honest. I liked his books before I knew anything about him. And then when I met him, he was nothing like I'd thought he'd be in person, and I was kind of disappointed—and that was before I knew he was a fugitive from one of the most famous prison escapes ever! But his original crime was holding up a bank with a toy gun, so it's not like he was a serial killer or anything, but does that make a difference?

"It's kind of messing with my mind. If you love something, like a book or a movie, and then you find out the person who created it did something awful or wasn't a very good person—is it still okay to love what they created?"

"Those are great questions," Miss Linden said.

"I think I'm wrestling with the same thing, James," Mr. Quisling said, "and I wish I had an answer for you. The only conclusion I've come to so far is that people are complicated, but that isn't a very satisfying answer."

"One thing that *is* satisfying about all this is finally getting an answer to a famous unsolved mystery," Miss Linden said.

"I agree with that," Lucy piped up, joining their conversation. "It's a great story. In fact, I e-mailed my editor to let her know I want to back-burner my Harriet Beecher Stowe book and write about Errol Roy instead."

"Oh, you have to!" Miss Linden said. "His story would be wonderfully told in your hands."

"You would postpone an entire book?" Emily asked, incredulous. "But you were so excited about Stowe!"

Lucy nodded. "And I still am. I know my work won't go to waste and something will come of it eventually. Sometimes stories aren't ready to be told. And sometimes stories don't *want* to be told. And that's not a bad thing. It's good to have something to wonder about."

"One thing I wonder," James interjected, "is if I need to take a break from Errol Roy mysteries for a while. I might need to branch out."

Hollister leaned into the group. "Did I hear somebody say they're in the market for new books? You're in the right place! If you like mysteries, have you tried Sammy Keyes? That's a great series. Or maybe *Winterhouse* if you like a little magic in your mysteries? Maybe *The Great Greene Heist* or *Belly Up*?"

Hollister kept pulling books off the shelves, and James's eyes got wider and wider as the stack piled up in his hands.

Mr. Griswold hurried over and put a hand on

Hollister's arm. "Don't pull too many of those books off the shelves, or you might disturb some of the setup for . . ." He lowered his voice and said, "The game."

"Another game?" Emily wasn't sure she could muster the energy to play another Garrison Griswold game so soon. She thought she'd need at least a week to unwind.

Mr. Griswold laughed. "It's a game I know you love, Emily. Book Scavenger! I figured we could do a Book Scavenger hunt in Hollister's store today. It will be a way for people to tour the different sections and have fun at the same time."

"Oh!" Emily brightened. "That sounds like a great idea!"

People began to trickle in for the grand reopening, and soon Hollister was tapping the service bell at the checkout counter to get everyone's attention. He stood on a chair and said, "I just wanted to say a few words before I hand this party over to my old friend Gary, who will lead you in another of his crazy games."

The audience chuckled and Hollister continued, "I can't say thank you enough to show my appreciation for all of you: my neighbors, my customers, and the bookseller community. When that fire got my store, I thought that was it. I'm old. Too old to start over. It wasn't how I wanted to go out, but we don't always get a say in that.

"And then the notes started to appear, and the crowdfunding was set up, and Binc—that's a bookseller thing, if you're not in the know—swooped in, and I just . . ." Hollister shook his head. "And these are people I know helping me, but also a lot of strangers.

"You can't lie down and give up when so many people are rallying for you. I appreciate it. And I wish for each and every one of you that you'll feel that rallying support when times get tough for you. You made that support easy for me to see—and you all know my eyesight has been failing, so I appreciate that very much."

The audience chuckled at Hollister's joke and he continued.

"If there are strangers out there who are rooting for me when I'm down, I know they are there for you, too. You may not see them or get the notes like I did, but I hope you believe there are more people wishing for you to succeed than there are hoping that you fail. I'm going to step up, rise up, and keep going because of you all. And if times get tough, I hope you'll imagine a team rallying for you, too, and step up and keep moving forward. Please stop by my store—you've always got a friend in me. And free Wi-Fi—we're going to have that now, too."

Everyone laughed at that. Hollister looked around for a glass to raise, but there wasn't one nearby, so he grabbed a bookmark from the stack next to the register and raised it in the air. "Cheers, to book lovers!"

Emily and the crowd returned his toast: "Cheers, to book lovers!"

After Hollister's grand re-opening had wound down, Emily and James went up the staircase in the back of the store to see what the new and improved loft looked like. There was a small couch and chairs, a colorful rug and cozy lamps, and, of course, books. Jigsaw puzzle pieces were spread across the coffee table for anyone to work on.

"James—the purple chair!" Emily pointed. It had been her favorite reading spot in Hollister's store before the fire, and she didn't think it had survived. She ran to it and collapsed in the seat, immediately realizing the feeling of the chair wasn't *exactly* the same. "I think this is a new one." She wriggled around a bit and rested her head back. "Still comfy, though."

"Check this out." James was inspecting a special bookcase designed to look like a potted bookcase flower. The flower part was a cabinet with a glass door attached to a post that had been secured inside a giant pot. Bookmarks sprouted around the post like grass, along with a sign that read *Take One! I'm Free!*

A sign on the front of the cabinet said *Neighborhood Reads*. Emily and James peered through the glass. Inside were two shelves filled with books. Each one had a notecard labeling one shelf "Quisling's Corner" and the other "Linden's Loves." Hollister's all-cap hand-writing explained, "These books are recommended to you by the winners of Garrison Griswold's Unlock the Rock competition on Alcatraz. Every month we'll feature different customer recommendations in this display."

They scanned their teacher's and the librarian's picks, and Emily pulled a book from Mr. Quisling's shelf called *Puzzle Mania*. Flipping through it, she said, "This looks cool. I'm going to get this with my gift card from Unlock the Rock."

She took the puzzle book to the purple chair and opened to a crossword puzzle. "A four-letter word for *square, clove hitch, sheet bend*," she read aloud to James.

"I know that! Thanks to my one year in the Boy Scouts." James plopped onto the couch next to her. "The answer is *knot*."

Emily tugged free the pencil tucked in her ponytail and filled out the answer.

"Were you disappointed we didn't win Unlock the Rock?" James asked.

"Well . . ." Emily traced a finger along a crossword row. "I'm glad Mr. Quisling and Miss Linden won. And I'm glad they figured out the solution in time for Hollister's store to get the bonus money. But it would have been great to win. Especially because we *did* figure out the answer."

"I know." James flopped back against the couch, disbelief written all over his face as he stared up at the exposed rafters in the ceiling. "If we hadn't hesitated over whether our answer was correct—"

"Or if Bookacuda and Fiona hadn't been trying to get us out of the game."

"Ugh," James groaned. "Don't remind me. That Bookacuda kid was the worst."

Footsteps clomped up the stairs, and they soon saw the green, lopsided Mohawk of Matthew. "Did I hear *Bookacuda*? Are you talking about his sabotage?"

"And Fiona's," Emily added. "We were saying we probably would have won if Fiona hadn't set you up to look like a thief and Bookacuda hadn't been trying to scare us with his notes."

"And stealing backpacks and messing up puzzles for other players," James added.

"Well, to be fair," Matthew interjected, "I kind of messed with him, too. Making up a fake puzzle only wasted his time. I mean, that was my intention, because he was always popping up and annoying us, and I didn't want him following us around, but I shouldn't have tricked him, either."

Matthew sat on an ottoman next to the coffee table and studied the spread-out puzzle pieces.

"Bookacuda deserved it," James said.

"I feel a little sorry for him," Emily said. "I checked his profile on Book Scavenger the other day and his account is deactivated now."

"Really?" James said, with surprise. "Because of the stuff he did at Unlock the Rock?"

"Not exactly. When word spread around the forums that he'd been disqualified from the game for cheating, questions came up about whether or not he'd genuinely earned his Sherlock-level status."

"How could he have fudged that?" Matthew asked, plucking a puzzle piece from the table and inserting it into the jigsaw.

James's eyes widened. "Did he hack into Book Scavenger?"

Emily smiled at his mind immediately leaping to computer programming. "No, I don't think so. People came forward and said he'd bullied them into finding books through Book Scavenger and letting him take credit on his Bookacuda account. Others said he paid them to hide or find books. I think hearing about Unlock the Rock triggered a bunch of people into issuing complaints against him, and it looks like either Bayside Press suspended the account or Bookacuda decided to deactivate himself."

"Why would you feel sorry for him knowing he treated other Book Scavenger players like that?" Matthew asked. "All that does is make me think he's even more of a punk than I'd initially thought."

"Well, I'd been surprised when I met him in person to see how small he is, because he was supposed to be an eighth grader. I'd chalked it up as another one of his lies, but he'd been telling the truth. Apparently, he skipped a grade at some point. In the Book Scavenger forums, kids from his school in Nebraska said he's always trying too hard to fit in and forcing people to be his friend. I don't know. . . . I just feel sorry for him." Emily grinned. "But only a little bit."

As different as she and Bookacuda were, Emily knew how it felt to want to fit in and to want a place where you felt you belonged, but they handled those feelings in totally different ways. Bookacuda seemed like the type who would elbow his way into a group shouting, "Notice me! I'm awesome!" Meanwhile, Emily used to hang back and watch a group, wishing she could be a part of them and hoping one day they'd notice her and invite her to join them.

James leaned over to scan the crossword still open on her lap. "Hey, look at this one." He tapped the page. "That's a good one for you: *Biblio larvae*."

"Oh! I've got it!" She adjusted her pencil and scratched in the letters to write out *bookworm*.

Matthew held out a hand, gesturing for the puzzle book. Emily gave it to him and he read through the clues silently. "Okay, here's one for both of you. And Errol Roy, too. *When a mystery is solved (two words)*."

Emily and James grinned at each other and said in unison, "Case closed."

AUTHOR'S NOTE

As with the first two books in the Book Scavenger series, *The Alcatraz Escape* is a work of fiction, but I drew much of my inspiration from historical people and events. The characters of Errol Roy and Lucy Leonard sprang from my imagination, but here are some of the factual elements that guided me in creating their stories.

ALCATRAZ

Alcatraz island is a prominent landmark in San Francisco, best known for the federal penitentiary that housed infamous convicts like Al Capone and the Birdman in the mid-twentieth century. The island has been utilized for centuries, beginning with the Native Americans who originally populated that area.

When the Mexican-American War concluded in 1848, Mexico gave the United States a large territory of land, which included the area that would become California, and in 1849, the American military determined Alcatraz island would be a prime location for protecting the San Francisco Bay. Plans to build a fortress began.

The citadel that Lucy Leonard talks about was a real part of the military fortress. It existed from 1859 to 1908, when it was torn down to make room for building a new prison. The new prison was built over the citadel basement, which had consisted of kitchens, dining halls, and storage rooms for water and food. Many of these areas are still accessible and they are sometimes referred to as "the dungeon" of the Alcatraz federal penitentiary. In researching this story, I visited the dungeon as part of a "Behind the Scenes" tour on Alcatraz, but much of the old citadel space was closed off from tourists, so my scenes set there are a combination of in-person observations, research, and imagination.

The U.S. Army also built underground tunnels for their use in the military fortress, although many of them are buried, if they continue to exist at all. In recent years, a team of researchers has been identifying the remains of these tunnels and other military-era structures with the use of radar. This is the "reconstruction" I imagined taking place in the story that had A-Block and the dungeon closed off. The federal prison morgue was built over an old entrance to a military tunnel but, as far as I know, that tunnel is not actually accessible from that location.

1962 ESCAPE

There were multiple escape attempts from Alcatraz, but the Anglin brothers and Frank Morris's escape in 1962 is the best known. The three men were all convicted bank robbers who spent months while on Alcatraz planning and coordinating their escape. They used their access to various prison facilities to stealthily make the props and tools that would aid them, such as a raft and life preservers sewn out of prison-issued rubberized raincoats, and dummy heads—decorated with real hair clippings from the barber shop—that were tucked into their beds on the night of the escape to trick any guard into thinking they were asleep in their cells. There was a fourth inmate, Allen West, who was supposed to join them that night, but he couldn't remove his cell grate quickly enough and was left behind.

What happened to the men after they launched their raft into the water remains an unsolved mystery. No bodies were ever found, leading to speculation that the men may have survived, although the FBI investigation concluded that their plan was a failure and the men drowned.

The story of this escape, the planning and intricacies involved, is fascinating and if you're interested in learning more I recommend reading *Breaking the Rock* by Jolene Babyak, who was a child living on Alcatraz, and whose father was the acting warden when the escape happened.

In addition to the 1962 escape, the character Errol

Roy was inspired by a line I read in *A History of Alcatraz* by Gregory L. Wellman: "The average prisoner read about 75 to 100 books a year, and the National Parks Service claimed that the prisoners 'read more serious literature than does ordinary person in the community.'" Roy's character was also influenced by Dashiell Hammett, who began writing detective mysteries after a brief career as a Pinkerton detective during his convalescence from tuberculosis.

HARRIET BEECHER STOWE

Much of what Lucy Leonard shares about Harriet Beecher Stowe is true: She was a mother of seven and a prolific writer, best known for *Uncle Tom's Cabin*, which was published in 1852 and became a fixture of the abolitionist movement. As Lucy says, Abraham Lincoln allegedly greeted Harriet Beecher Stowe at a White House reception in 1862 by saying, "So you're the little woman who wrote the book that started this great war!"

Frederick Stowe was the fourth born of Harriet Beecher Stowe's children. He was eleven when *Uncle Tom's Cabin* was published and his mother was catapulted to fame. Frederick struggled with an alcohol addiction beginning at age sixteen. Between 1861 and 1865 he served in the Civil War in various infantries. In 1871 he boarded a ship headed for San Francisco. He wrote Harriet when he arrived in the city and mentioned plans to go to sea, but was never heard from again and his whereabouts remain an unsolved mystery.

The rest of Frederick's story I created. There was no letter in Mark Twain's belongings, and I imagine the possibility of a letter from Frederick Stowe getting mis-delivered to Twain would be unlikely, as Harriet didn't become Twain's neighbor at Nook Farm until two years after Frederick had disappeared, but I thought it made for a good story.

ACKNOWLEDGMENTS

Creating a book is something that feels simultaneously mundane and magical. I sit by myself in a room and type—mundane. This finished book you are holding in your hands—magical! It is a group effort that makes the magic happen, and I have immense gratitude for the following people who helped bring *The Aloatius Escape* to life.

My editor and publisher, Christy Ottaviano, who always seems to understand the story I'm trying to tell better than I do myself. We've now created three books together, and every time, I marvel at the finished product. I feel so lucky to be working with you.

To my literary agent, Ammi-Joan Paquette, thank you for your steadfast support and encouragement, your brilliant eye for story, your kindness and friendship—I could go on and on, but in short: thank you for being awesome.

A group hug to the entire *Book Scavenger* team at Henry Holt and Macmillan for all the care and attention you have devoted to this series, including Jessica Anderson, Lucy Del Priore, Molly Brouillette Ellis, Katie Halata, Morgan Rath, April Ward, and

Melissa Zar. A special shout-out to the production team for *The Alcatraz Escape*, especially production editor Starr Baer and copyeditor Karen Sherman, who worked wonders in a short amount of time and over the holidays.

Thank you to Sarah Watts for your fabulous illustrations. Discovering how you will bring scenes and characters to life is always a part of this process I look forward to.

To my dear Writing Roosters, thank you for helping me unravel this story. Your friendship means more to me than I can adequately express.

Thank you to the many people who answered questions for me as I researched various aspects of this book. At the risk of forgetting someone with whom I had a conversation that was instrumental in developing this story, I want to thank US Marshall Michael Dyke; George Durgerian, park ranger with the Golden Gate National Parks; Sylvia Rowan, San Francisco History Center librarian; Liz Austin and Bruce Creamer; Kristin Poirier and Mark Wolfman; Vanessa Harper; and my dad, Tom Chambliss.

Thank you to my friends and family for your encouragement, support, and enthusiasm for my books, and for being understanding when I've had to hunker down in Book Scavenger land.

Thank you to my son, who fills every day with light and laughter (and trains and Legos and superheroes), and to my husband, who is the best partner a writer could ask for. *The Alcatraz Escape* would not have been finished on time without your unflagging support and belief in my abilities.

And to all the readers, young and old, who have embraced Emily and James and have been eager to read another Book Scavenger adventure—thank you, thank you, thank you.